Open The Box

and other stories

Andrew Humphrey

Elastic Press

ISBN number: 0-9543747-1-1

Printed by Anglia Digital Print, Norwich. Tel 01603 414443.

Typeset by Angela Hook

Earlier versions of some of these stories have appeared in
the following: *The Third Alternative, Crimewave, Hidden
Corners, and Roadworks.*
They have been edited for this collection.

Elastic Press are currently seeking submissions for future
single author short story collections.

Published by:
Elastic Press
85 Gertrude Road
Norwich
UK
ElasticPress@elasticpress.com
www.elasticpress.com

For my sons, Graham and Simon

With thanks to Andrew Hook and Andy Cox

Table of contents

Open The Box

She barely registered when I first saw her. I turned the corner from the stairway onto the top floor of St Stephen's multi-storey and there she was; standing with her back to me, leaning against the safety rail, bare hands on the cold metal. She wore a black woollen overcoat that was too big for her and scuffed Doc Martens. The wind caught her hair, which was wild anyway and so dark I thought it must be dyed. She blew smoke from a roll-up into the January air. I followed her gaze. It was hard to tell where the cold concrete and steel of the car park ended and the sky began.

I found my burgundy Mondeo and dumped my shopping in the boot, then hesitated by the driver's door. The girl and I were alone and there was something odd in the way she stood and stared at nothing but the grey middle distance. I thought I should say something; but I was cold, I had a sore throat. I wanted to lock myself in the car, turn up the heating and listen to Coldplay on the stereo as I drove home.

As I opened the door the girl stepped onto the parapet, straddling the safety rail. She steadied herself then lifted her other leg over the rail and leant back against it, balancing awkwardly on less than a foot of concrete.

Her head tilted upwards and her eyes were closed. She wasn't pretty. I frowned and wondered if that mattered and found I wasn't sure. Her face was white, her lips thin. Her features sharp and angular.

I walked towards her. The smell of urine drifted across from the toilet by the lift. "What are you doing?" I said. Hardly original I know, but by now I felt as though I was on autopilot; as though I was still standing by my car, leaning back against it, arms folded, bored, watching it all unfold.

"Hazard a guess," she said. Her voice was light, indifferent.

She didn't look around. "Don't come too close. I'm going to jump anyway, but I don't think you want a front row seat. Know what I mean?"

I'd already stopped. I looked around, listening for footsteps on the stairs. I wanted this to be someone else's responsibility. Five minutes earlier, five minutes later and it would have been.

"Aren't you supposed to try and talk me down?" She sounded almost amused.

The wind that scurried amongst the concrete and steel was cold and I thrust my hands deep into my pockets. Her back was to me and I knew it was futile but I shrugged anyway. "Well, I'd rather you didn't, but..." my voice tailed off. I found myself thinking about the shopping in my car, wondering how long it would take for the frozen food to de-frost.

She turned at my silence. Her eyes were green and they shone with a curious light. "Hey, I'm sorry if I'm boring you."

I snapped back into focus. "God, no. Look, I'm sorry..."

"Forget it." She closed her eyes, exhaled slowly then turned back to face the drop. "It doesn't matter. It's all bollocks anyway. Sorry I've fucked up your day. Do me a favour? Tell my mum she's a bitch and I hate her guts."

She stepped forward and dropped out of sight. I heard nothing except the wind and the muted growl of the traffic below. I didn't rush to the rail and look down. Eventually I fumbled the phone from my coat pocket and dialled 999.

"It was her choice," Jenny said, handing me a mug of coffee and sitting in the armchair opposite. She sat with her feet splayed and her knees touching. She leant forward and looked into my face. "I suppose it was her right, actually. Don't you think?"

I sipped my coffee and said nothing. I've found with Jenny that's often the best way. This week her hair was dyed dark red and parted in the middle. She kept tucking one side behind an ear; the other hung across her left cheek, casting it in shadow. She wore a biscuit-coloured roll-neck sweater with a fawn skirt and dark brown woollen tights. Autumn personified.

She leant across, put a hand in my hair, tugged at it gently. "Answer me."

"I choose not to." I looked into her soft brown eyes and she smiled.

"You're learning, Steve. You've changed a lot."

"For the better?"

"Of course. If today had happened a year ago imagine the state you'd be in. You'd have dissolved. You'd have probably followed her down."

"Instead I was just bored. Annoyed. Worried about the state of my shopping. The poor cow even apologised for fucking up my day. That's progress, I suppose."

I felt her eyes on my face but I wouldn't meet them. I put my mug on the coffee table. We were in Jenny's flat near the city centre. It was early evening and dark outside. We were snug in the lamplight with the curtains drawn.

I sat back and let my breath out slowly. The sofa was old and lumpy; mustard Dralon covered with a patterned throw that smelled of pot. "According to the police her name was Julie. Julie Patterson."

"Does that matter?"

"I expect it matters to her mother."

"And do you know her mother?"

"You know I don't."

"So why does it matter to you?"

"Not tonight, Jenny. For Christ's sake."

She smiled and ran her fingers through her hair, pulling it back, away from her face. Her features changed as they emerged from shadow.

"I'll be off," I said. "It's been quite a day."

"I thought you'd stay."

"Not tonight."

She stood, folding her arms. She was a little shorter than me. Twenty-three years old. Pretty, most of the time. "We haven't slept together for over a week."

"Jenny, three hours ago I watched a girl commit suicide. I'm really not up for a shag."

She shrugged. "Sex and death. I thought it might get you going."

I put on my coat. "Goodnight, Jenny," I said.

"Oh, God. Rejection. How will I cope?" She smiled as she spoke, even laughed a little. But her eyes wavered on my face.

*

We'd met four years earlier when Jenny had temped at the insurance company where I work. One of the underwriters had left unexpectedly and his supervisor discovered a pile of unprocessed proposal forms in his desk drawer. Jenny and I spent a week clearing the backlog. Her hair was blond then, tied back in pigtails. She wore short skirts and bright make-up and too much perfume. She made me coffee and bought me King Size Mars Bars. She looked me in the eye when I spoke and listened to every word. I wasn't used to that.

I was twenty-four and recovering from a broken engagement. Jenny got the whole story. She made the right noises at the right times and said that Karen was a fool to let me go. I suppose I lapped it up. She left on the Friday and we agreed to go for a drink over the weekend.

When Jenny opened the door to me on the Saturday evening I thought I'd got the wrong flat. Her hair was jet-black, cut very short. She wore a baggy purple sweater with a pleated skirt, black leggings and trainers.

"Oh," I said.

"What?"

"Nothing. You look different."

"And?"

"It's a bit of a surprise."

"Good. Surprises are good. Don't you think?"

"Sure."

"Right." She looked suddenly serious and glanced at her watch. "Decision time."

"What?"

"We can go to bed or nip around the corner for a pizza. Your choice. You've got five seconds. Go."

I stared at her open mouthed as she counted the seconds down.

"Time's up," she said. "Call me tomorrow." She shut the door in my face. I stood there for ten minutes, knocking occasionally, then gave up and went home.

I phoned the next day and got no reply. I was determined not to call on the Monday but by 10.30 in the morning I had. I went to her flat at lunchtime, not knowing what to expect. We drank coffee and talked for hours. At least Jenny talked for hours. It was like a dam bursting. An erratic dam at that, as she flitted from subject to subject without warning. I was bewildered, but intoxicated. Occasionally she'd lean across and slip her tongue into my mouth and kiss me slowly and deeply for perhaps five minutes before withdrawing and talking again as though nothing had happened.

We went to bed, eventually. I was dazed and lost and Jenny took the lead. The bedroom was damp, the sheets clammy. Jenny guided me and teased me and came at me from all angles and it was more like a battle than making love. She was on top when I finally came. She leant over me, ran her fingers through the sweat on my chest. I felt as though I'd been drugged and beaten.

*

It was Saturday lunchtime when I met Carol Patterson, four days after her daughter's death. We sat in the corner of the Horse and Dray on Ber Street; near a fruit machine and an open fire, opposite the French windows that led to the walled off area that was popular in the summer. She'd telephoned me the previous evening. The call had surprised me and I agreed to meet her without asking why or thinking it through.

4

She was a short woman, about fifty, slim, with a thin face, hollow cheeks and startled blue eyes. Her hair was her best feature; it fell in chestnut curls to her shoulders, softening the sharpness of her face.

She thanked me for seeing her and we made some stilted small talk. She took a deep swallow of her gin and tonic. She put the glass precisely on the beer mat and ran a finger through the beads of condensation. Her hands showed her age the most; veins blue and prominent through the thin skin. Her nails were immaculate though; carefully shaped and painted.

Finally she got to it. "I spoke to the police about Julie's final moments. They told me about you, obviously." She looked at her glass as she spoke, tilting it so that the ice cubes clinked together. "Apparently Julie said nothing before she jumped. You walked towards her and before either of you could say anything she went over the edge."

"That's right," I said. I felt my cheeks colour slightly. I drank some lager.

"I don't believe you."

I looked up in surprise. She'd seemed timid, incapable of confrontation. "Why should I lie?"

She shook her head. "I don't know. Don't care. I'm not trying to trick you or accuse you of anything. You're my last link with Julie, Mr Rose." She paused, glanced up at me again. "Steve. My last link. She didn't even leave a note. She must have said something. Perhaps it didn't seem important at the time. It must have been difficult for you. You were in shock, I expect."

Her voice had an edge to it. A whine. The need came off her in thick waves.

I looked into my drink. "She said she loved you."

"What?"

"Look, I'm sorry. You're right. I was in shock. She said, tell mum I love her and that I'm sorry."

"No she didn't."

I kept looking down and said nothing. A chocolate Labrador gazed balefully at us from beyond the French window, it's expression almost comically sad.

"Julie was a drug addict. Heroin mostly. In and out of rehab since she was fifteen. Her dad left us a couple of years earlier. I blame him. Easier than blaming myself, isn't it? The last time she told me she loved me she was twelve years old. God knows I've tried to help her. But last week I simply couldn't take anymore. I found out she'd been stealing from me. It wasn't

5

the first time, but this was so cold, so systematic. And she was back on heroin, of course. She swore she was clean, but it was just another lie. So I kicked her out. Tough love I think they call it." She was quiet for a moment, her thoughts wandering. Then she composed herself and looked into my face. "So, tell me what she said. Please."

I told her. She nodded.

"Thanks for getting there. In the end."

She talked some more about Julie and I nodded occasionally, not really listening. We finished our drinks. She asked me if I'd like another and I said no. Then she surprised me. "Can I see you again?" she said.

"What?"

"I'd like to meet you again. To talk."

"Why?"

"I said before. You're my last link with Julie. I can't just let that go." Her eyes were wide, her voice uncertain.

"I don't think so."

"Please." Her need was almost tangible and it revolted me.

"No. It's not going to happen. It wouldn't help either of us." I spoke more sharply than I intended. I thought of Jenny, of how she would approve.

Carol's face trembled. She stood and swept past me without speaking. I didn't look back and moments later I heard the door open then close. She left only the heavy scent of her perfume and an empty glass with lipstick prints on the rim.

*

It was a weekday, the first February after we met that Jenny and I drove to Cromer in my new Mondeo.

"Am I supposed to be impressed by this?" she said.

"What?"

"The new car. The penis substitute. Do you think it'll make me wet?"

"It's just a car," I said mildly. "You're generalising again."

"Don't patronise me." She turned her head away; her face set in a determined pout. But she looked beautiful that day. She'd let her hair grow out into its natural colour; a sort of dirty blond. She fixed it in a ponytail with a crimson scrunchy. Beneath her dark coat she wore a simple black woollen dress with black stockings and high-heeled shoes. When I picked her up that morning I said she looked edible and she told me to grow up.

"You're nineteen, for Christ's sake. You can't tell me to grow up," I said, offended.

She looked up at me for a long moment then and I thought she was going to hit me, or cry, or both.

In the end she said quietly, "You can be an arsehole sometimes, Steve," and walked out to the car.

It was cold and clear inland but when we hit Cromer the front and the beach were coated with a thick, freezing fog.

Jenny brightened immediately. "I love it. The way it distorts everything. Sound. Distances." We paused at the bottom of the concrete ramp that led to the beach and Jenny slipped off her shoes and handed them to me.

"You'll freeze," I said.

"Well, you'll just have to warm me up then, won't you?" she said, slipping an arm in mine and leaning against my shoulder.

I pulled her closer. I felt a knot in my stomach loosen.

We ate fish and chips at the Cromer Grill and on a normal day we could have seen the sea from our table. But today fog pressed up against the window and tendrils of it eased into the restaurant's warmth whenever the door was opened. The fog smelled of vinegar and crabs and cold salt.

Later, we found a second-hand shop a couple of streets away. Jenny headed straight for the books. They occupied one corner; a mix of hardbacks and paperbacks sprawled in random piles.

"They're only 50p each," Jenny said, kneeling among them. "Look. James Lovegrove. Nicholas Royle. Excellent."

I smiled. I was about to join her when I saw the pile of shoes that filled the opposite corner. According to a hand written sign they were a pound a pair. Not that they were sorted into pairs. They were in a single heap, as random as the books. Odd children's shoes emerged; pink, yellow, bright blue. I squinted at them, squeezing the colour out, seeing them in black and white.

I closed my eyes and turned away. The elderly lady behind the cash register was regarding me curiously. She was smoking a cigarette that looked and smelled French and knitting something long and pink.

Belatedly I realised that Jenny was calling me. She was holding some books up for my inspection and grinning.

"Yeah, great," I said. "You take your time. I'll wait for you outside."

She followed me through the door. "What?" she said.

"Nothing," I said. "What happened to your books?"

"Fuck the books. What's the matter?" She linked her arm in mine and we walked slowly.

"It was those shoes," I said. "It probably sounds

stupid. I visited the Auschwitz museum a couple of years ago. There was a glass case full of shoes. Twenty-five thousand pairs. That was one days worth, Jenny. One day. Can you imagine that?" I could. Indeed had, often. "It reminded me of that. It's something I often think about. Dream about, even. It upset me a bit, that's all."

We walked for a while in silence then Jenny slowly pulled her arm from mine. "Are you a Jew, Steve?" she said quietly.

"No," I glanced at her uneasily.

"Any Jewish friends? Anyone you know whose relatives were caught up in the Holocaust?"

"No. Why?"

"Then what the fuck were you doing visiting Auschwitz? It's none of your business." She stopped and turned towards me. The fog had lifted a little and the fury was clear on her face. "Those shoes upset you, did they? It's something you think about, is it? Well that's big of you, Steve. Those kids have been dead over fifty years. All your thoughts, all your upset, what iota of good have they done?"

"Fucking hell, Jenny..."

"Shut up. You're a self-indulgent wanker, Steve. I'm catching the train home. I wash my hands of you."

She turned on her heels and walked into the fog. It was three months before I saw her again.

*

A week after Carol Patterson walked out on me in the pub Jenny and I sat on a bench next to Pull's Ferry and fed stale bread to the ducks and geese and watched the Yare's cold green water ebb against the bank. The day was clear and cold and thin sunlight sparkled off the river and Jenny's eyes shone with dark refracted light. As so often happens on still days in Norwich the stink of chemical shit drifted across the city from the sewerage works at Whittlingham.

"Is she still ringing you, then," Jenny said, tossing the last of the breadcrumbs onto the river's edge then clapping her gloved hands together to clear the debris.

"Every night," I said, "and at work. I've tried to be reasonable but I ended up putting the phone down on her yesterday."

"Poor cow's probably after your body. You should give her a break."

I looked across at her. She stared straight ahead and her face was empty. Occasionally we heard the roar of the crowd from the football match at Carrow Road.

"Look, I feel sorry for her, but frankly it's not my problem. I thought you'd approve. You taught me all I know, after all."

She put her hands to her mouth in mock-horror and for the first time that day there was a trace of animation in her voice. "Oh my God. I've created a monster."

On the far side of the bank, to our left, a line of three anglers sat motionless, hunched forward, breath turning to smoke in the cold air. Raucous ducks surrounded our feet and a pair of blue tits hovered at their periphery.

Jenny and I had met only twice in the last ten days and kissed just once, at her instigation. Even then she'd withdrawn quickly, sensing my hesitation. I hadn't missed her. As I sat next to her on the cold bench, with her cute in her beige bobble hat and sleek brown coat with matching boots, I realised that a large part of me would rather have been at the football match half a mile away.

I thought for a moment then looked across at her. "Jenny, I think we should stop seeing each other."

She paused, not looking at me. "I can't hear you," she said. "It doesn't count if I can't hear you, does it? That's what we used to say at school." She shot me a crooked smile, one I didn't think I'd seen before.

"We've not been close recently, have we?"

"Whose fault is that?"

"I don't think blame is helpful," I said, following the conventions doggedly, eyes cast down, not even particularly interested anymore.

"Don't look so worried, Steve. I'll live. I don't even mind that much. I miss the old Steve."

That got my attention, as I suppose she knew it would. "That's a bit rich, isn't it? Considering the old Steve is in there," I said, pointing at her stomach. "You swallowed him whole."

"You took me so seriously. I was only nineteen, what the hell did I know? I was just fucking with your head. But you took it all, didn't you? Jumped through hoops. Changed yourself because I said so. It was a bit of a rush, actually. At first." She gave me that crooked grin again. There were spots of colour high on her cheeks and her eyes were bright. I looked away from her and said nothing.

"Don't worry," she said, "I'll never darken your doorstep again."

"Jenny."

"Good old Steve. Still can't take a joke. Actually I've got a chance of a job away. In Manchester."

"Christ. You'll need your passport. What is it? Still with the BBC?"

She nodded. "I suppose I might as well take it."

"It sounds good."

"You don't have to look so relieved."

"I'm not," I said quickly.

She laughed. "It doesn't matter. It's all bollocks anyway."

I looked at her sharply then but her expression was blank. I started to say something but she stopped me. "Please spare me that crap about still being friends."

"Right," I said. "But there's no-one else, you know. If that matters."

"Don't flatter yourself, Steve. I don't care. You are now, officially, in the past."

She stood and kissed me primly on the forehead. Her lips were cold. She walked off in the direction of Riverside. I watched her briefly then looked away. A pair of geese squabbled noisily on the far side of the river.

*

After Jenny abandoned me in the Cromer fog we spoke on the telephone a handful of times; drab conversations, Jenny speaking in a bored monotone while I fought to keep the desperation out of my voice. It was May before we met. It had rained heavily the day before but the Saturday I walked to her flat it was warm and bright and the air fizzed with the scent of fruit and new leaves gathering on wet trees.

She didn't look surprised to see me. She ushered me in without speaking.

"My turn to surprise you," I said.

"It's only taken you three months."

"But you told me to keep away."

"So I did," she said. She seemed bored and she wouldn't look at me. "And as usual, you believed me."

Her hair was short again and vaguely pink. She wore a yellow cotton dress and white sandals. I could see the outline of her knickers through the dress and she wasn't wearing a bra.

"Have a good look, why don't you," she said and I turned my head away, blushing.

"How about if I had a man here?"

"What?"

"You heard me."

"Have you been seeing other people?"

"That's my business. And it's not the point."

I stood with my face burning, wondering what the hell I was doing there.

"What's that? A present?" she said.

I was carrying a shoe box and she was looking at it.

"No. Not a present. More like a confession."

I put the box on the coffee table and removed the lid. Jenny sat in the chair next to it and peered inside.

"Newspaper cuttings," she said, pulling a handful of papers out of the box and leafing through them.

"Mostly from The Guardian and Observer. Stuff off the Internet as well. I expect you think it's sick."

She looked slowly through the cuttings and said nothing. They were mostly articles and photographs relating to the Holocaust, but some concentrated on executions of Partisans in Poland and Czechoslovakia in the early years of the war. The photographs were stark and graphic.

"I thought about what you said in Cromer. About Auschwitz. You were right. It's misplaced pity. Something to hide behind. An excuse to feel sorry for myself." I pointed at the box. "I've been collecting this stuff for about five years. I look through them every month or so." Suddenly, stupidly, I felt close to tears. "I don't know why."

"Why give them to me?"

"I mean I don't get off on this stuff or anything. I empathise with the victims. I'm not some Hitler groupie." I put my hands to my face and rubbed my eyes hard.

"Why give them to me, Steve?"

"I want you to burn them. I want you to help me put this behind me. I want you to help me change, Jenny." My eyes were hot. I knuckled them again.

"I can't give you absolution, Steve," she said, then shrugged. "Just lighten up. Don't take yourself so seriously. Don't take me so seriously. Stick the box in the bin."

"No. You take them, Jenny. It's important."

She gave me an odd smile, her head tilted to one side. She stood and picked up the box. "Come with me."

I followed her into the bedroom. She opened the wardrobe and put the box in the corner, on the floor and covered it with an old sweater. "There," she said, "out of harms way."

"Thank you."

She smiled at me again. This time there was a hint of warmth and I felt my pulse quicken. "You're a strange one," she said. "What am I going to do with you?"

I said nothing. I could hear my heart thump in my chest. She pulled the straps of her dress away from her shoulders and let it drop to the floor. Her nipples looked dark and hard and I remembered how they felt in my mouth.

She stepped out of her knickers. "We've got some catching up to do," she said. She smiled her odd smile and held her arms out towards me.

*

Jenny and I met just once more before she moved to Manchester; at her flat on a damp cold Sunday morning. We handed back books and CD's that we'd lent each other. She had more of mine than I had of hers and I told her not to worry about it, but she insisted. There was something ritualistic about it, I suppose. And an air of finality.

We spoke little and when we did we were unnaturally polite. She said she'd met someone called Guy and he was cute and there was talk of him joining her in Manchester at some point. I said I was pleased and found that I meant it.

I was glad to leave. Jenny seemed smaller somehow, more rooted in the usual dimensions. I walked home through streets that were drab and grey, but I caught myself whistling and smiling at people that I didn't know.

The next weekend I watched Norwich City draw nil-nil with Barnsley at Carrow Road. I was numb with cold long before the end. It was a poor match. Barnsley were muscular, Norwich gormless. I thought of Jenny sometimes, but not that often.

The Friday after I tried one of the plethora of clubs that had sprung up on the Riverside development. I spent the evening and the early hours of the next morning drinking vodka and Red Bull and attempting to hold shouted conversations with people I'd never met before and didn't particularly want to meet again. I ended up pissed and wired. The next two days passed in a grainy, monochrome haze.

Some time in early spring when all was calm and smooth and my life seemed to belong to me and to nobody else I found myself in front of Carol's house on Bluebell Road. It was a redbrick semi-detached with a glass porch. Winter jasmine laced the trelliswork on top of the fence. I knocked without thinking and when she answered I didn't know what to say. Neither did she and for several interminable moments we gazed awkwardly past each others shoulders until she ushered me inside.

12

"This is a surprise," she said. Her eyes were the startling blue I remembered but dark flecks seemed to swim in them now. She didn't smile.

"I wondered how you were," I said, attempting a grin that was meant to be disarming, but probably fell a long way short. "I'm sorry about...before. I feel bad about it."

"Do you?" she said. Her hair was straighter and shorter. She wore a navy sweatshirt and a knee-length skirt. Her shoulders slumped and her features relaxed. She pushed the living room door open. "Come on through. I'll make some tea." She smiled. "It's good to see you, actually. Despite everything."

We ended up drinking tea in the kitchen, sitting opposite each other at the chunky pine table. "It's me who should be apologising," she said. "I lost it badly. I had no right to pester you like that."

I mumbled something and drank some tea. Carol talked about Julie for a while; how she'd coped since the funeral. I pretended to listen and nodded occasionally. "And I'm seeing someone. I've known him for years. It's not serious and it's not exclusive." She looked at me as she spoke. "And how are you?"

I shrugged. "Oh, fine. Great, really."

She kept looking at me. "How's Jenny?"

I paused. I couldn't remember telling her about Jenny. I could have asked her about that, or told her to mind her own business. I could have smiled and ignored the question. I think that's what I meant to do. Instead I looked up at her and spoke for perhaps fifteen minutes, barely pausing to draw breath, about Jenny and I. How we met and how we'd ended. How it was Jenny's fault that I'd treated Carol so thoughtlessly. It just gushed out. Like bile. I glanced up at Carol occasionally but she kept her expression blank. When I finished she said, "And you miss her?"

I laughed. "Christ, no. Too much like hard work. I'm much happier now."

She nodded slowly. I stood and she put a hand on my arm. "Can I show you something before you go?"

I nodded.

I followed her upstairs. On the small landing she paused outside a white panel door. "This is Julie's room," she said, almost reverently. "I've kept it just how it was."

How original, I thought. She pushed the door open. It was my turn to keep my expression blank. It wasn't much of a shrine. A single bed covered with a beige patterned blanket. Pale emulsioned walls dotted with sporadic posters of Placebo and Mansun. Generic bedroom furniture. A few cuddly toys. A radio. The scent of old pot.

Carol sat on the bed with her back to me, her hands smoothing the blanket on either side of her. I thumbed through some paperbacks in a dark wood bookcase. There were several Terry Pratchett's and I looked up to ask her something and I saw that her shoulders were shaking.

I moved towards her, extending a hand. I said her name. She let out a braying sob, turned slightly, took my hand and pushed it against her hair. "Come on," I said, moving closer. She pressed her face against my stomach. I could feel her heat through my cotton shirt. Her face was level with the waistband of my jeans. Her sobbing subsided. "I'm sorry, Steve," she said.

I stroked her head and said nothing.

"Don't go yet," she said. Her voice was thick, clotted.

"Carol," I said.

I felt her undo the lower buttons on my shirt and pull it open. I closed my eyes as she nuzzled the soft flesh around my navel. "Oh, shit," I said.

I took her from behind on her daughter's bed. She was on all fours, skirt hitched up, tights and knickers yanked down, bunched above her knees. She howled when she came and I wondered if I was killing her. I'm not sure what noise I made but the intensity of my orgasm astonished me. My knees buckled and I fell against her. I thought I could smell her sweat and her need but it might well have been my own.

After we'd cleaned up we could barely look at each other. We made it downstairs somehow and when I stepped out into the brightness of the day the air felt cool on my burning cheeks.

I was on her doorstep again the next evening, just before dusk. Carol looked tired when she opened the door and she shook her head.

"Fine," I said, with my head down. But I didn't move.

"Oh, shit," she said, and reached for me.

We went to Julie's room again. Same bed, same position. Same tights and knickers for all I know. Same orgasm.

She didn't answer the door the next time I called, a couple of days later, although I was sure she was in. The same thing happened the next day and the day after. Her telephone was permanently engaged.

On Saturday I answered my door to a bearded, middle aged man who said his name was Dave and he was a friend of Carol's. I didn't invite him in. He looked wretched and couldn't meet my eyes and mumbled so badly that I had to ask him to repeat himself. "You've got to keep away from Carol, man."

"My name's Steve."

"Whatever. Don't call. Don't visit. She'll call the police if you do. I don't know what happened between you two; don't want to know. But she's really fucked up. You've got to give her a break." He spoke quickly, through gritted teeth, trying to get it over with.

"No problem."

He glanced up at me. "You're cool with that?"

"Yeah. I'm cool. Man. What? Do I look desperate?"

I thought I saw a flash of anger then, but it didn't last long. He looked down again, shook his head, walked away from me.

I closed the door and went into the kitchen. I smashed all my drinking glasses, one after the other, against the tiles above the sink.

I phoned in sick on Monday. Said I was running a temperature. By Wednesday I was and I lay on the sofa, wrapped in my quilt, watching daytime television. It was the end of that week that Jenny sent the shoebox back; wrapped in brown paper with a Manchester postmark. There was a note attached. She couldn't bring herself to burn it, she said. But she couldn't keep it. She often found herself looking through the contents and thinking of me. I wasn't sure what to make of that.

But I spent an hour browsing through the cuttings. They felt like old friends.

*

Saturday evening I sit at my kitchen table with that day's Guardian spread in front of me. The shoebox is open on a chair by my side. I settle on an article that caught my eye earlier. The headline reads, "What Daddy Did In The War". It deals with the enthusiastic complicity of ordinary Germans involved in atrocities throughout Europe during World War II. Two photographs sit in the middle of the text. The first shows a greatcoat clad Nazi officer placing a noose around the neck of a young woman. The officer is clean-shaven and smiling. The woman is probably little more than a girl. She is pretty, with blond curly hair, wearing a blouse and a cardigan and a skirt.

Her hands are tied behind her back. She gazes with no expression at a point somewhere beyond the camera. Just to the side of her, noose already in place, is a strikingly handsome boy with thick dark hair. He smiles straight at the camera.

The next picture, presumably taken minutes later, shows the aftermath. The officer is out of shot. The girl and the boy hang, their heads angled towards one another. According to the caption this is the execution, by the Gestapo, of members of the Resistance in France in 1941.

I stare at the photographs for a long time. I touch them, run my fingers across their surface. I wonder what their names were; the boy; the girl; the officer; whoever stood behind the camera. I wonder what they thought and felt in those last moments. Perhaps if I stare hard enough I can pull myself back to that French dawn. It will be as grey and cold as steel. I wonder on which side of the camera I'd be.

At last I sit up, rub my eyes. I cut the pictures out and put them in the box.

How Much Do You Want To Know

The day my brother died the wind was mild and from the east and what clouds there were seemed high and thinly spread. It was March impersonating May. My brother and I looked across the line of sea barley at the angled, understated coast and heard the cries of the Fulmers and the Black-Headed Gulls wheeling above us.

It was a good day, the kind of day that had been common years ago, but less so since I'd married Kate. David was single.

He was quiet through that afternoon, but then David was often quiet. He had dark hair and a serious face and startling, ice-blue eyes that were difficult to read. His smiles were minuscule and hard earned. To call David wry would be an understatement.

My car was parked near Blakeney town centre and we made our way back to it.

"Just like the old days," David said.

"Hardly," I said. He wore a shirt and tie, although it was a Sunday. I thought of what Kate would say and looked away from his earnest face. "Only one of us can remember the names of all the birds, all the flora. And fauna. In Latin."

"It's a gift," David said, his face flat.

"Well, I admire it. Mind like a sieve, me."

"Yeah, I'm a real wow at parties." His hair was receding slightly. He ran a hand through it. In retrospect perhaps his face was paler than usual, the dark rings under his eyes more pronounced. Perhaps. Or maybe I'm imagining it now. Knowing what I know.

I climbed into the driver's seat, slammed the door shut, gunned the engine.

"Seatbelt, Martin," David said. I sighed. I think he smiled a little.

By the time we reached David's terraced house on Ashby Street it was almost dark and it had become noticeably colder. David's house, shabbily unkempt from the outside, looked bleak and unwelcoming. "I'll come in for a bit, if you want," I said. "You can make some tea. I'll pretend you've got some chocolate biscuits."

"What?" he said. "No. Thanks. I'm tired, Martin."

I think he looked at me then. I'm not sure. I was too busy scrabbling at my feet, retrieving a cassette I'd dropped earlier. "Jagged Little Pill" by Alanis Morrisette. "See you, then" I said. I heard the car door open. Looking back I try to imagine that I felt something, some frisson, some mild premonition. But that's bollocks. I barely spared my brother a passing glance as I steered my car back towards Queen's Road.

I didn't know David had a gun. It wasn't until much later that I found out where he got it from. It was a shotgun. Double barrelled, although the barrels were sawn off. About an hour after I left him, at least that's the Coroner's estimate, he sat on the floor in his kitchen, pushed the stunted barrels of the shotgun under his chin and pressed both triggers. It almost blew his head off.

"He was your brother," Kate said. "I'm sorry you've lost your brother."

"You should audition for the speaking clock. The job's yours." She stood by the coffee table in our living room. She folded her arms and shivered.

"I won't pretend, Martin. I loathed David. You know that. That hasn't changed because he's dead." I looked hard at her but she kept her head cast down, her eyes fixed on the TV guide that lay open on the table. It was the evening before my brother's funeral and the wind outside whined and nibbled at the drawn curtains, even though the window was closed.

"So you're not coming, then?"

She closed her eyes and sighed minutely. "No. I think I've made that pretty clear."

We spoke as though we were strangers. Kate's features, pretty as they were, looked hard and angular, her eyes were hooded in the lamplight.

"I don't know what mum will say." I sat at the dining table. The remnants of our evening meal were spread before me.

I picked up my wineglass and peered at the residue in the bottom.

"Actually, Martin, I think she'll understand." Kate's voice seemed infinitesimally softer. I looked at her again but didn't speak. I wanted to rewind a fortnight. Or fast forward six months or so. I just couldn't stand it where I was. I hated the wretched, stultifying misery. I'd been a toddler when my dad died. This was the first grief I'd known. And I wanted my wife back. I loved her, needed her even. I had no idea where she was.

"I'd thought you would pretend. For my sake." I ran a finger around the rim of the glass. I could smell the cold bolognaise sauce congealing on a plate by my elbow. My head ached.

"That's not my style, love." I jumped slightly. She'd moved to my side and put a hand on my shoulder. "You're the one who pretends, remember. I pick up the pieces. I have to see things as they really are." I touched her hand. Her fingers were cold. So were mine, I expect. The heating had turned itself off and there was a chill in the room. "I know what a cow I'm being. You're a sweet man and I love you. Remember that." Her voice was softer still now, but distant.

"Despite my faults?"

She smiled briefly, stiffly and met my eyes for the first time since God knows when. "Because of them, perhaps."

My mother hardly spoke at all until after the funeral.

We were alone in her small council flat. It was early afternoon and watery light struggled through the kitchen window. She took her gloves and coat off and laid them on the table. She smelled of lavender. She smelled of old piss as well but I tried not to notice that. She stood at the window with her arms at her sides. She seemed shorter than ever. Her grey hair was freshly permed. I filled the kettle with cold water and tried to think of something to say.

I arranged cups and saucers on the kitchen table. "Sit down, mum."

As she sat she reached automatically for the biscuit tin, set it on the table, slid it towards me. I took out a chocolate digestive, looked at it, then put it back again. "I'm sorry about Kate," I said. I sat opposite my mother and studied the coarse grain on the pine table.

"Why?" she said. Her voice was flat, her face set in the same blank expression that she'd worn when I'd told her that David was dead.

"She should have come. Whatever she thought of David. It's not like her."

"It's exactly like her. She's not a hypocrite, Martin. Not like me." She looked into her tea. She must have known that my eyes were on her.

"What do you mean?"

Her eyes were bright and dry. "I only went today for your sake."

I let her words sink in. "What are you talking about?
David was your son. You loved him."

"He was my son, yes. But the only person who loved him
was you, Martin. Ever. But you couldn't see it. Still can't.
I'm sorry for you."

The kitchen was cold and her breath turned to smoke in
front of her. I stood and stuffed my hands into my pockets. I
blinked rapidly. "I don't get this. So he was a little odd. Big
deal. He wasn't a murderer, was he? Or a child molester? Perhaps
he was, you just forgot to tell me?" I found it hard to swallow.

"Don't be foolish, Martin."

"He was my big brother and I loved him." My voice broke
then. My mother drank some tea and put the lid back on the
biscuit tin.

"Go home, Martin. Patch things up with Kate. You need
her now."

"Patch things up? Kate and I are fine." There was a long
pause. "Have you been phoning her again?"

"We call each other. Quite often. She's a good woman."
She bit her lip.

"Better than I deserve?" I said. "Is that what you were
going to say?"

She shook her head and stood and put the tea things in
the washing up bowl. I stared at her back for a long while,
clenching and unclenching my fists. Then I left.

It was after Christmas that the dreams started. In them
I was younger, I'm not sure what age, but I was tiny in a vast
bed in an oversized room the walls and ceiling of which towered
way above me and met at odd angles. It was just me and the bed
and the long, distorted shadows of something just beyond my
eyesight. Nothing happened. I'd track the shadow's progress
around the alien room. I'd feel the slow swell of terror build
in my chest. I'd wake stifling a scream, my back and chest slick
with sweat, the quilt clenched tight around me. Occasionally
Kate would stir. Sometimes she'd hold me, sometimes not. I never
mentioned the dreams to her and she never asked. They came once,
perhaps twice, a week for six months. Then they stopped.

It was spring, just over a year after David's death,
when I met Grace, one of his former colleagues, in a pub just
outside the city centre.

"It was good of you to come," I said as we took our seats
at a wall table. She nodded and sipped her orange juice. She

looked terrified, I thought. A young woman with features just the right side of plain and long black hair and glasses that tried, and failed, to hide startled, jade green eyes. She kept smiling nervously and tucking strands of her hair behind an ear.

"I'm not sure how much use I'll be. I hardly knew David. None of us did. He kept himself to himself."

"I know," I said. I drank some lager and tried to gather my thoughts. "This seemed like such a good idea. But now I'm here I don't know what to ask."

"David was good at his job." She glanced briefly at the door. "But beyond a 'good morning' or a 'good night' we hardly spoke at all."

"Did he have any friends at the library?"

"Frankly, no. It's not that he was rude or unpleasant, he simply wasn't interested in conversation." She fiddled with her hair again, touched the rim of her glasses, splayed her fingers on the table and examined them.

"No girlfriends, then?"

She almost laughed. "God, no." A hint of colour crept into her cheeks. "I'm sorry. No offence."

"It's ok."

She put her hands in her lap. "A couple of the younger girls used to tease him. At least, they tried to."

"About what?"

"They thought he might be gay. They tried to get a reaction."

"And did they?"

She gave a small smile. "Not for a moment. He completely ignored them. Actually, I quite admired him then."

"And how about you, Grace? Did you think he was gay?"

She looked indignant. "I neither knew nor cared. It was none of my business. It still isn't."

It was my turn to blush. "No. I'm sorry."

"And what difference does it make, anyway?" There was animation in her voice. "Honestly, in this day and age."

"You're quite right, of course. It makes no difference. No difference at all." I drained my glass. Grace finished her orange juice and said she didn't want another. I was glad when she left a few minutes later. I had another drink. I sipped it slowly and thought about my brother, about all the lives he hadn't touched.

It was summer. My mother sat in a wicker chair on the patio that led out to our garden. I stood by her side. I could see Kate through the french windows, clearing the dinner things from the table. The glass of the window distorted her. When she looked in my direction I didn't recognise her face at all.

"Bailed you out again, has she?" my mother said. She was squinting at the heat haze at the bottom of the garden.

"Not exactly," I said. "I've got a few cash flow problems, that's all. I'll pay her back."

"Like you did before." I said nothing. "Oh, I'm not criticising, Martin. You had the good sense to marry someone who had a rich father. Good for you. It's a gift. Recognising your limitations." She spoke mildly, her hands folded in her lap. She seemed smaller than ever. Withered. Desiccated. She smelled of nothing at all. Even the stink of piss had gone. I almost missed it. I saw that Kate was standing completely still, watching us. "If only David had possessed your sense."

"What?"

She seemed surprised that I had spoken. "If he'd found someone. Somebody like Kate. Somebody to hide his weaknesses."

"What weaknesses?"

She snorted. "What's the point, Martin. You'll deny it. It's how you get by." She turned her face slowly up towards mine. I imagined driving my fist into it.

"I haven't got a fucking clue what you're talking about."

She turned away from me again, her shoulders stiffening.

"That's right. Resort to profanity. I'm not criticising. At least you get by. Unlike David. Or your father."

"My father? What about my father?"

"Nothing. That's what he amounted to. What they all amounted to. Nothing." Her face darkened as she spoke. Then it darkened further as Kate's shadow fell across it.

"Everything ok?" she said. "I could hear you two through the window. You mustn't upset yourself, Eve. Everything's fine, isn't it, Martin?" Kate's skin was translucent in the sunlight. She had her hair up. Her skin was flawless. She looked appallingly beautiful, I thought.

"What? Yes. Wonderful. Bloody wonderful."

Kate gave me a smile of sorts. My mother stared past me, her eyes wet and empty.

Once, when I was twelve and David eighteen, we visited our father's grave.

"Why is he buried here?" I said. David parked his old Escort in a parking spot close to the centre of Long Stratton.

We walked to the church.

"It's where we used to live," David said. "Before you were born."

"You never said. Nor did mum."

"She won't mention it. It's the past, isn't it? It's dead, like dad. As far as she's concerned we never lived here, dad never existed."

His expression was serious, as usual. It was summer and he wore a sweater and a tweed jacket and I could see the sweat on his face and neck. "I don't understand," I said.

"You're not meant to."

The headstone was as simple as it could be. A name. Some dates. That's all. We stood there for a while, our faces empty. Neither of us had brought flowers.

I was hot and thirsty and the smell of the long grass made me want to sneeze. "How did he die, David? Mum's never told me."

David stood with his hands in his pockets. His face was pale, his eyes dry. He squinted against the sunlight reflected off the church and the clean, new headstones.

"Do you remember him?" I said as we walked back to the car.

"Of course I remember him." He spoke sharply and a moment later he put a hand on my shoulder and I flinched slightly. "He was ill, Martin."

"Ill? What, cancer? Something like that?"

"No. Not really." He spoke slowly. "He hanged himself in his study. Because he was ill." I blinked twice quickly. David stopped. "That's wrong. Completely wrong. Mum killed him. She didn't kick the chair away, but she may as well have done. She made him ill." His voice had an edge to it I hadn't heard before and his face had changed.

"I don't understand. I don't like this, David."

"She's infected." He hissed it, leaning forward, eyes narrowed. Then the heat fell from his face and his eyes widened briefly and he shook his head. "I didn't say that. Any of it. You never heard it from me."

"David?" I was close to tears.

Then he held me. It seemed shocking, him touching me. Anybody touching me. I felt his bony chest against mine. My arms stuck out behind him. I didn't know what to do with my hands. Then he let me go and we walked to the car and drove back to Norwich.

During the summer Kate had an annex built on the side of our house and in the autumn my mother moved into it. I can't remember it being discussed. It just happened. One Tuesday morning when Kate was off doing her voluntary work my mother and I found ourselves together in the kitchen. We weren't alone often. By design, on my part at least. Mother scrapped butter on a slice of wholemeal toast while I made myself coffee.

"Are you out today?" she said. "Any work to go to?"

"Not today," I said. Nor this week, I could have added. This month. She nodded slowly and took a tiny bite of toast. The kitchen was warm and her arms and legs were bare. I could see the outline of her bones through the thin skin.

"I gave him the gun," she said. She chewed her toast, kept her eyes on the teacup by her left hand.

"What?"

"I think you heard. It was his father's. I thought he'd like it."

"Like it?" My hand was frozen inches from the kettle. Steam boiled around my bare arm. I scarcely felt it.

"He was always asking about his father. It seemed appropriate."

"Dad was supposed to use the gun, wasn't he?"

She shrugged. "He didn't have the guts."

I realised that my arm hurt. I switched the kettle off and pushed it to one side. "Why tell me this?" I spoke to myself. "Why the fuck are you telling me this?"

I think she moved. I don't know. I couldn't look at her. "Why not?"

"What do you have for me? A knife? Some poison?"

"Foolish boy. You're different. You have Kate."

As winter pulled in Kate and my mother would spend most evenings sat in opposite chairs in our living room. They'd speak in low voices and watch television occasionally. They sat in shadow, a single lamp on, the curtains drawn. My mother had shrunk further and Kate, although slimmer, more angular than ever, seemed taller and chillingly beautiful. But I couldn't tell them apart. I looked hard into the half-light, but I could distinguish nothing. Even their voices blurred together. I could make out a hand occasionally, reaching, touching an arm, another hand. I heard laughter from time to time, brittle and brief. And I kept my distance.

It's Christmas Day, I think. I neither know nor care. It's dark outside. And in here, mostly. Shadows are puddled everywhere. I can't remember it being any other way. I can hear them as always. Low, insistent voices. But it's different this time. I've heard my name. Two, three times. I didn't recognise it at first. But now I'm curious. I move closer. I smell something. Something familiar. I'm not sure what.

They sit in a dark pool. "Martin? Come closer." I do as I'm told, but I still can't see anything. And the voice could be anyone's voice. Anyone at all.

A hand juts out of the darkness. I peer at it. It should be obvious whose hand it is. A young woman. An old woman. The difference should be clear even to me. But as hard as I peer and squint I simply have no idea.

The fingers strain towards me. "Take my hand, Martin. There's a good boy."

I frown. "I'm not a child," I say. My voice shocks me. It's little more than a whine. Perhaps I am a child.

The fingers splay open. Maybe they grow a little. I take the hand. It grips me tightly and I know that it will never let go.

Burning Bridges

"Is it genuine?" Graydon said.

Charlie clipped the video back into its plastic case. "Too right," he said. "One hundred per fucking cent. Fucking gold mine, mate." His eyes shone. Graydon recognised the greed on Charlie's face. He saw it on his own most mornings when he shaved.

"How do you know? They can make anything seem real these days," Graydon said. Charlie's flat surprised him. Neat. Newish furniture. Tastefully lit. He'd expected something more in keeping with Charlie's reputation; sordid, low rent. A slum, in fact.

"You saw it. It was shot in one take. No tricks," Charlie said. Graydon just looked at him, arms folded, until Charlie shrugged and looked down and said, "we did some checking, right? At least Macy did. He traced the guys who made it. Where do they come from? Latvia? Belarus? One of those old Soviet states, anyway. It's the real thing, Mr.Graydon. And there's more to come. I tell you, those fuckers out there, they just don't give a shit."

"They just happened to speak English, did they?"

Charlie sighed and shook his head and sat on the edge of the pale lemon sofa. He was short and skinny and although he was barely in his thirties his hair receded at the front and he wore it long at the back in a vain attempt at compensation. He wore a t-shirt and jogging trousers and Graydon could see old track marks on his arms. He'd heard the rumours that Charlie was clean now; that Macy had grown tired of him injecting their profits and Graydon thought the rumours were probably true. Charlie seemed pretty together. Repulsive, but together.

"Look, Mr.Graydon, you came looking for us, remember? Macy said it was fucking serendipity or something. We need to cut someone in. We know that. Duplication, distribution," he shrugged, "not our scene. We're small time drug dealers, right? So we need help. But you've been out of the business two, three years? We can find someone else."

Graydon smiled. "Of course you can. But it's pissing you off, isn't it? I can see it in your face. You think you're so close, don't you? To real money."

Charlie necked some beer from the bottle of Beck's on the nicely understated coffee table. "I don't get it. Why bother coming over here? Why watch the film if you're not interested?"

"I didn't say I wasn't interested."

"Macy said you were a pro. He did some business with you years ago. Thinks the sun shines out of your arse. Fuck knows why."

"Where did you get the film?"

"What difference does it make? You're just jerking us around. You'd better fuck off before I lose my temper."

"I'm shitting myself," Graydon said. He stood at the end of the table; tall, broad, densely muscled.

Charlie shifted in his seat. He held the beer in both hands. "It's a genuine snuff movie. We could make a fucking fortune."

"Did you really think I'd want a cut of that filth?"

Charlie looked up at him with his mouth open. "What's this? Mr.Morality? Porn paid for your Jag. How many houses have you got? Four? Five? Fucking hypocrite."

"Nothing like that," Graydon said, pointing at the video. "Just wank films. Suck and fuck. No kids, no animals." He picked up the video and held it close to Charlie's face. "And no snuff."

"Right. Whatever. We'll find someone else." Charlie tried to smile, tried to sound as though he didn't give a shit, but Graydon could see the fear on his face. He sat on the sofa, close to him, so that his own muscled thigh pressed against Charlie's much thinner one.

"What did you think of it? The film. How did it make you feel?"

Charlie tried to shrug but Graydon's shoulder blocked him. "Nothing. It's just cash to me. Big house. Decent car. Proper women for a change. It was my big break."

"You're lying. I was watching you. I saw it in your eyes. You got off on it, didn't you? You liked the money shot best, didn't you? Blood and spunk. Bonus."

Charlie tried to stand but Graydon held him easily.

"And what about the woman, Charlie? What did you think of her?"

"What do you mean?" Charlie looked around him, his eyes wide. He stared at the Christmas cards on the mantelpiece. Graydon had noticed them before. He'd been surprised by how many there were. He thought maybe Charlie sent them to himself.

"It's a straightforward question. The woman you watched them murder. What did you think of her?"

Charlie shook his head and tried not to whine. "Nothing. Nothing. She was just a junkie. A prostitute. Probably both. Did you see the state of her? They did her a favour. She was old too. Thirties, forties even. Come on, man. What the fuck is it to you?"

Graydon stood and examined one of the Christmas cards. A fat Santa was stuck in a chimney. "She was my sister," he said.

Charlie swallowed. "But you haven't got a sister."

When he turned back towards Charlie Graydon was smiling and there was a gun in his hand.

Charlie swallowed again. "Oh fuck. Macy said you had no family. It's what gave you an edge, he said. You had no-one to give a shit about."

"She was only twenty-eight, actually. I must admit she looked older. In and out of clinics since she was fourteen." Graydon shook his head slowly. "She's been such a worry. She's why I got out of the business. I tried to look after her. But she ran away six months ago. The last I heard she was looking for work somewhere in Eastern Europe. That was three months ago and I've heard nothing since. Nothing."

"It's a fake," Charlie said quickly. "We were trying to con you. She's fine. Leave it to me I'll trace her for you. She's fine, Mr.Graydon."

"That's bollocks. We both know that." He became aware again of the fear on Charlie's face and saw that he was staring at the gun. "Don't worry about this," he said. "I'm not going to hurt you. I just need some information."

"Right, right. You need Macy, man. He sorted it. I don't know anything."

"Where is Macy?"

"He's in Glasgow. He's got family there. I think he's doing some business as well. He'll be back after Christmas."

Graydon smiled. "Thanks, Charlie."

Charlie smiled. Graydon shot him twice in the face.

*

It was a week into the new year before Craig Macy returned to Norwich. Graydon met him in Earlham Park. It was a Wednesday morning, early enough for the mist to linger in the branches of the bare trees and to cling to the reeds on the riverbank.

Macy was a big man. Bigger than Graydon, although not

as fit. His stomach lolled over the waistband of his faded jeans. He wore a flannel shirt and an unzipped fleece jacket. He had a beard and unruly fair hair.

"I can't find Charlie," Macy said. "I think the little bastard's done a runner.

"I'm not happy about being stood up," Graydon said.

"I'm sorry, Mr.Graydon. I just don't get it. There's no sign of the film either. What's the stupid little shite think he's going to do with it? Flog it to Blockbuster's?"

"Don't worry about Charlie," Graydon said.

They followed the riverbank, walking slowly in the direction of the University. They stopped at a small clearing. A handful of ducks scattered. Macy sat on a wooden bench. He put his head in his hands.

"I've let you down, Mr.Graydon."

"Nonsense, Craig. And call me Paul."

Macy looked up.

"We go back a long way, don't we Craig?"

Macy nodded.

"You sold those video's for me, remember? Must be seven, eight years ago. Did me a big favour."

"You did me the favour, Mr.Graydon....Paul. I needed the money."

"You did some time though, didn't you? Three months wasn't it? And you kept your mouth shut. Never mentioned my name at all, the way I heard it."

Macy smiled and shrugged. "It was nothing."

"I've never forgotten. I should have repaid you years ago. But now I can, can't I? I can sort this mess out for you."

"How? What about Charlie?"

"I told you not to worry about Charlie. He's way out of his depth." He looked at Macy's big, open face. He saw hope in his eyes. And admiration. Graydon had to look away. "Just tell me where you got the video from. Leave the rest to me."

"Moscow."

"That narrows it down."

"I've got names and addresses. You know Steve Hooper? He owed us big time. Gave us the tape as a down payment. Reckoned he picked it up on a business trip."

"Did he know it was genuine?"

"Yeah, but it meant nothing to him. He was in a bad way. He owed money all over the place. He was hooked on speed and coke and skag. D'you hear they fished him out of the Thames about a month ago? He'd been shot in the head."

"I heard."

"Could have been anyone. Could have been the Russian's for all I know. When he said he picked the tape up I get the impression he helped himself."

Graydon pulled a pad and a pen from his coat pocket and tossed them onto Macy's lap. "Write it all down, Craig. Everything you know. Then leave it to me."

"You going out there, Mr.Graydon? You'd better be careful. They're mean bastards."

"So I hear. Just write it all down, Craig."

Macy wrote slowly, his tongue sticking out of the corner of his mouth. When he finished Graydon pocketed the notebook. He stared out a swan as it swam past. He felt the gun in his pocket. There were three bullets left in it. He didn't like guns.

"Have you seen the film, Craig?"

Macy grimaced. "Yeah. Poor wee lassie."

Graydon nodded and breathed heavily. "Oh, Samantha, what the fuck have you done to me."

Macy frowned. "Who's Samantha?"

"No-one you know."

"Are you all right, Mr. Graydon?"

"No. I think I'm losing it." He looked at the concern on Macy's face and shook his head. "I don't need to do this. Burning bridges and all that."

"What's up, Mr.Graydon?"

"Nothing that need concern you, Craig." Graydon said, then pulled the gun from his pocket and emptied it into Macy's chest.

*

Later, Graydon drove to Heathrow. He used his mobile to book a one-way ticket to Moscow's Sheremetyevo airport. In the car's boot he had a holdall with a change of clothes, a couple of sweaters and a quilted Parka. He thought Moscow might be quite cold. Beyond that he had no idea what to expect. He found he didn't care. He didn't think he'd be coming back. He wasn't at all sure that he wanted to. He smiled as he hit the M25 and it started to rain.

A little later a black cab pulled away from Norwich Airport. The woman in the back was twenty-eight although she looked about a dozen years older. She was skinny with dark hair. Her eyes were sunken.

She lit a cigarette. The driver said, "It's a no-smoking cab, love." Then he half turned and saw the utter, used exhaustion on her face and said, "Forget it. You go ahead."

She smiled. At least he thought it was a smile.

Carved in Water, Not In Stone

I parked my silver Mondeo in a passing spot on a small road just
outside Mulbarton and watched the low September sun ease like warm
butter across the wheat field to my left. I keyed a familiar number
into my mobile phone and paused with my finger over the send button. After a moment I cancelled the call and tossed the phone and
my suit jacket onto the back seat. It's a company car. I'd be happy
with a Toyota or a Nissan. I don't care about cars much. I sat
there for another ten minutes or so, thinking about things I don't
care about, thinking about pretty much nothing at all. Then I
started the car and pulled out into the empty road.

Julie was waiting for me in the usual place. She had her
arms crossed in front of her and was looking at her watch.
"You're late," she said, belting herself into the
passengers' seat. "I was about to give up on you."
"Sorry. Work. You know how it is."
She wouldn't look at me. She was in her mid-forties,
which gave her about ten years on me, with long black hair tied
back in a ponytail. She was slim and pretty and wore a cream
blouse with a tight black skirt. There was a hint of grey in
her hair and if you looked closely you could see the lines on
her neck and the beginnings of crows feet under her eyes.
She lit a cigarette.
"I thought you'd given up," I said.
"I had," she said.
I wound the electric window on her side down a fraction.
I could smell her perfume. It was different from usual,
something light and floral. It made me want to sneeze.
She blew her smoke out into the early evening. Country
smells filtered in. Grass, animals, manure.
"Are we sitting here all night?" she said.
"No." I pulled my tie down and loosened my collar, then
put the car into gear and drove off.

Usually we'd drive to the copse behind the derelict farm
off the Mulbarton Road or, on the few times that her husband
was away, to Julie's house in the next village. But I drove on
past our usual turn, heading into the depths of Norfolk.

Julie looked at me sharply. "Where are we going?"

I shrugged. "I'm not sure. I thought we'd just drive for a while."

"Drive?"

"Give us a chance to talk for a change."

She laughed humourlessly and flicked her cigarette out of the window. I wound her window up and turned the air-conditioning up a notch. "Sorry, Chris. Conversation? I never took that for your strong point." Julie said. Then after a pause, "No offence."

"None taken."

"I mean if I want conversation I'll talk to my husband."

"Yes, I think I take your point."

She lit another cigarette and crossed her brown legs. "Wifey found out, has she? Or have you discovered your conscience at last."

"It just seems a little undignified, that's all. Wrestling in the back of a car. We're not teenagers anymore, are we?"

"Hypocrite. A few weeks back you couldn't get enough of it. You thought it was exciting, as I recall. Liked the risk of getting caught."

I shrugged. "Anyway, the cricket season's nearly over. I've no other excuses for getting out every Thursday."

She said nothing, just sat with her arms crossed and stared out of the window. I took a left turn. It felt hot in the car in spite of the air-conditioning and the steering wheel was slippery with my sweat.

"We can still see each other," I said.

"What the fuck for?" Julie said

"Look, I'm sorry.."

"Don't flatter yourself, Chris. Don't go getting the idea that I give a shit. You'd better drop me at the usual place."

Twenty silent minutes later I did. She walked away from me, hips swishing defiantly. Typically, I started wanting her again then, when she was way out of reach.

*

I drove around for a while with the windows down and let the evening air displace the scent of perfume and cigarettes.

When I got back to our semi-detached on the outskirts of Norwich a little before ten Rebecca was in the living room watching a video. I was rooting around in the kitchen and she called through to me. "Did you win?"

34

"What?"

"The cricket?"

"Oh. Yeah, we won. I scored thirty not out. Took a couple of wickets as well."

"You've had a good season."

I frowned to myself. Perhaps I'd overdone it a little. If I'd really shown the form I'd claimed during my imaginary season I'd be on the verge of international recognition. I took a plate of cold chicken and salad into the living room.

Rebecca sat on the sofa. She was wearing a pink dressing gown and matching slippers. Her dark hair was wet and she smelt of soap and talcum powder and her lips were warm when she kissed me on the cheek.

"Perhaps you should think about playing weekends next season," she said.

I grunted noncommittally. "How's your mother?" I said.

"About the same. Dad'll ring if she gets any worse."

I nodded at the TV. "What's this?"

"Sixth Sense."

"Is that Bruce Willis? In more than a vest?"

"Actually, he's quite good in this."

"First time for everything."

She told me about her day as I ate. She's a supply teacher and she had a couple of weeks at a grotty school looking after a class of psychotic eight year olds. "They're good kids, really," she said at one point. Right. Rebecca likes to think the best of people. She'd probably say the children from "The Village of the Damned" were basically decent kids at heart.

The film ended soon enough. Later we made love and, later still, after Rebecca was asleep, I crept downstairs and studied the next days horse racing in the evening paper.

*

On Friday morning the office was hot and stuffy and the day seemed to stretch ahead endlessly. The computer monitor in front of me blinked without pity. The report I was writing stubbornly refused to sort itself into any kind of order. By drinking coffee and gossiping I lasted until just after three. Then I told Janet, on reception, that I had a doctor's appointment and that I'd be back Monday.

The Ladbroke's on White Lion Street was less than ten minutes away. Ray was behind the counter as usual and he nodded at me laconically. I was just in time to put twenty quid on the favourite for the ten past three at Haydock. It won at five to two.

"That's better," I said, partly to Ray, mostly to myself.

By a quarter past five I was just under a hundred and sixty pounds down. The horses were gathering at the start for the final race of the day, a sprint handicap at Thirsk. I really liked the top weight; he had won his last two races and was well drawn. But the only money I had left was fifty pounds I'd borrowed from petty cash earlier in the week to pay for a lunch that was subsequently cancelled.

I shrugged and wrote the ticket out. Twenty-five pound each way at six to one.

"It's certain to get at least a place," I said to Ray. He gave me the look of someone who's heard it all before. I ignored him and leant against the shop's central pillar and watched the race.

My horse's good draw became a liability as he missed the break and the rest of the field hampered him in their bid to reach the favoured stand rail. He never recovered. In the final furlong he ran on past beaten horses to finish fifth or sixth.

"Shit," I said, tossing my ticket on the floor. I didn't look at Ray. When I stepped outside I had to shield my eyes against the brightness of the day.

*

On Saturday Rebecca visited friends and I spent the afternoon chasing the previous day's losses. I stopped at a cashpoint before lunch and withdrew two hundred pounds from my current account. That took me up to my overdraft limit less than halfway through the month. I intended to put fifty pounds away to cover the petty cash I'd lost, but by four o'clock the whole two hundred had gone.

I picked up Rebecca and we drove home through the city. After a few minutes she asked if I was all right and I said I was. "You're quiet," she said. I shrugged.

Then she said, "Oh, Chris. I don't get paid 'till next week. Can you sub us some cash? For housekeeping and stuff?"

"What now?"

"Today or tomorrow. It's not a problem, is it?"

"'Course not. But a little notice would have been nice."

She turned to look at me. I could feel the heat rising in my face. "What's the matter, Chris? What aren't you saying?"

"Nothing. For Christ's sake. I'll get it tomorrow."

She turned away from me again and stared out of the window, her hands clenched in fists in her lap.

36

Sunday morning I told Rebecca that I was popping to the cashpoint then drove to Gordon's house instead. Gordon was a workmate and one of my few friends. I persuaded him to lend me fifty quid. It wasn't easy. It wasn't exactly the first time I'd asked.

"You're doing it again, aren't you Chris?" he said

I couldn't look at him. We were on his front doorstep and I could hear his young daughter laughing in a back room. "'Course not, mate. I'm just in a bit of a hole, that's all. You'll get it back next week."

He wasn't happy but he lent it to me anyway. When I got home I gave the money to Rebecca and she took it without speaking.

*

At work on Monday morning I found Gordon and thanked him again. He gave me a look I couldn't read and said, "The old man wants to see you. I think you're in deep shit."

"What's new," I said.

David Baxter's office was bigger than it needed to be and was as neat and well ordered as the man himself. He was in his late fifties, pale and lean with grey hair that was conservatively cut. It was widely accepted that he was good at his job, that he worked hard and that he had the personality of a tree stump.

"Good weekend, David?"

Baxter had a blank A4 pad in front of him and he doodled on it as he spoke. "I needed you Friday afternoon, Chris. Where did you get to?"

"Doctor's. I told Janet."

"There was nothing in the diary."

"It was a last minute thing. Bit of a chest infection. A few antibiotics and I'll be right as rain."

"Glad to hear it. I needed the Ashford site investigation Friday. I had to get Neil to finish it over the weekend and deliver it to the client first thing this morning."

"I thought I had until Wednesday."

"I usually make my deadlines pretty clear, Chris."

"Yeah. I'm sorry, David. What can I say?"

He stared at the pad for a moment, admiring a series of diminishing circles that he'd just drawn. "I know that you're gambling again, Chris."

I waited for some emotion to surface. Fear, apprehension, shame. But there was nothing. "I'm not sure that's any of your business."

"Ordinarily I'd agree. I know where you were Friday afternoon, and most other afternoons for that matter. I think that's company time, don't you?"

I didn't say anything.

"How many chances have I given you?" Baxter said. I shifted forward in my seat and stared at the floor. "And I need that fifty quid paid back into petty cash. All the receipts have got to go to head office."

"Right," I said. "I've left it at home. I'll sort it out tomorrow."

Baxter put his pen down, sat back in his chair and looked at me until I met his gaze. "I'm going to have to let you go, Chris."

"I see."

"No more chances."

"Shouldn't I get a written warning or something first?"

"We can do it that way if you want. Or you can leave today and I'll pay you for three months and give you a decent reference. Otherwise I'll have to resort to the truth."

"Whatever."

"I've heard some other stuff about you as well, Chris." This time he avoided my eyes. "I don't know if it's true or not."

He paused as though expecting an answer.

"Well, that really isn't any of your business, is it David?" I said.

He looked as though I'd slapped him. I stood and pulled my car keys out of my pocket. "What do want to do about these?"

He looked up at me. "Oh, fuck the car, Chris," he said, "just get out of my sight."

Gordon came up to me as I cleared my desk. "Proud of yourself?"

"Give it a rest, Gordon. Since when did you give a shit what the old man thinks?"

"You don't get it. He's stuck his neck out for you how many times? He's a decent bloke and you've kicked him in the teeth. And it's not just that." He ran his hands through his hair. "You know how I feel about Rebecca."

"Hey, easy tiger. You're a married man, remember?"

"How do you live with yourself? You're screwing around again, aren't you?" He shook his head. "How can you do it to her? It's like kicking the shit out of a puppy."

"You've made your point. What do you want me to do? Open a vein?"

"Just think, Chris. Try and think just what the fuck it is you want. If you feel like rejoining the human race then fine, otherwise just piss off and leave us all alone."

His face was red and for a moment I thought he was going to hit me. For a moment I wanted him to.

I walked home slowly. Autumn was kicking in early, the breeze had an edge to it and the first leaves were gathering on the pavement.

The house was quiet. Rebecca had a day off because of teacher training and usually when she was at home during the day she listened to music or the radio. Today it was like a morgue. She sat at the kitchen table, her face the colour of paper. She didn't seem surprised to see me.

"I've got some stuff to tell you, Rebecca," I said.

She looked up at me briefly and nodded and I sat opposite her and told her everything. I told her about the third mortgage I'd taken out and how I'd forged her signature to get it. I told her the full extent of my overdraft and the money I owed to family and friends and a variety of credit card companies. I told her about the job. And I told her about Julie.

Rebecca sat and took it all without flinching. I looked at her and wondered who I was and what the hell I was doing.

I finished and we sat in silence for minute. Then Rebecca said, "Someone put this through the letterbox this morning."

She handed me a white envelope. I pulled the letter out and read it. "Oh," I said.

"Someone doesn't like you," she said.

"I had no idea. I'd made my mind up to tell you anyway. I didn't know someone would beat me to it."

"It doesn't matter." she said. "If I'm honest with myself it wasn't that much of a shock."

"I haven't been that careful. Everyday I thought you'd find out."

"You wanted me to know. Equally I couldn't accept it. I didn't want to believe you could do it to me all over again."

I made us some coffee. It gave me something to do and it meant I could avoid her white face and the dark hurt in her eyes.

"Look, Chris, can you go for a walk or something? I'd like to be on my own for a bit."

"Of course," I said.

I walked for over an hour, scarcely noticing where I was going. My self-absorption was so complete that when my mobile phone rang it took me a moment to realise what it was. I pulled it from my pocket and pressed the appropriate button. I hoped it was Rebecca. But it was a man's voice, one I hadn't heard before.

"That's Chris, is it? Christopher Webb?"

"Yes," I said.

"You don't know me. But you know my wife. Julie. You know her pretty well from what she told me."

"I take it you're Brian, then. Julie mentioned you. She said you had an understanding."

"Oh, we do. At least she thinks we do. It's not that I give a shit what she gets up to, but it pisses me off the state she gets into when her little affairs crash and burn. I'm always picking up the pieces after some heartless bastard and this time it's you."

"I take it that you sent the letter to my wife."

"That's right. I spared her some of the details. It's hardly her fault, after all. I've had an agency keep tabs on you the past month or so. I sent the whole dossier to your boss. Didn't waste any time, did he? Not that I blame him. You're a bad man, Chris."

"Can't argue with that. I want to thank you, Brian. You've done me a favour."

"That's right. Put a brave face on it."

"I'm serious. If you were here I'd shake your hand."

"Are you taking the piss?"

"Perhaps a little."

"Enjoy it while you can. Your job's gone and your money. Give it a month or two and it'll be your wife who's fucking someone else."

"Perhaps. Perhaps not."

He laughed unpleasantly. "Get your head out of the sand. You've had your chances. All I did was finish you off. In the end I didn't even enjoy it much."

"I'm touched, Brian. But instead of worrying about me perhaps you should give some thought to your own life. Oh, and give my love to Julie," I said and broke the connection.

A minute later the phone rang again. This time it was Rebecca. "Can you come home, Chris? Now."

She was in the living room, standing by the French windows, looking out at the garden. She was even paler than she'd been earlier and her eyes were red.

"Shit. What have I done now?" I said.

She managed a smile. It almost broke my heart. That surprised me a little as I didn't think I had one.

"Not everything is about you, Chris. It's mum. She's had another stroke."

"Shit, I'm sorry," I said.

"I've got to go. I'm meeting Jill at Liverpool Street Station and she'll drive us to mum's."

I nodded.

"You'll need this," she said, handing me the fifty pounds I'd given her the day before. It seemed like a hundred years ago. "You'll need something to live on. Of course you can stick it on a horse and go hungry for a few days if you want. It's up to you. I've phoned the school. I'll use my Barclaycard for the train fare and stuff. Everything else can wait until I get back." She shrugged and looked out of the window again. "I don't care much about money. Never have."

She packed quickly and called a taxi.

"Give your parent's my love. And your sister, of course."

She nodded. "I'll probably ring in a couple of days or so. You'll either be here or you won't. It's up to you. Your choice. No ultimatums. In the end we do pretty much what we want, don't we? And we fool no one as easily as we fool ourselves."

She kissed me before she left. There was warmth in the kiss as well. I marvelled at that long after she'd gone.

Less and Less

"Don't go," Daniel said, and watched Helen's back stiffen.

She paused in the microscopic adjustment of her lipstick for a moment and said, "I've got to go, Daniel. I'll be late." She hesitated, then left it at that. Daniel knew what else she wanted to say; they had a mortgage to pay. It wouldn't do for her to lose her job as well.

He sat at the kitchen table, toying with a piece of burnt granary toast. He could see her in the hallway, in front of the full-length mirror. She looked crisp and efficient in her navy suit and dark tights. Her blond, highlighted hair was perfect, as was her make-up. It took her around an hour and a half to prepare for work each morning. Daniel had timed her. And on this particular morning he'd kept count of the number of words she'd spoken to him. Thirty-four.

"Phone in sick," he said, knowing she wouldn't. "I need you here. I thought you understood." He sounded like a child. He knew how much it irritated her, but he couldn't help it. That or he enjoyed it. He wasn't sure which.

She sighed and turned towards him, her blusher, mascara and lipstick finally applied to her satisfaction. Her prettiness was sharpened, defined. He preferred her without the mask. First thing in the morning, vulnerable, eyes soft with sleep. But it had been a long time since she'd cared what he thought.

"Sarah will be here soon." She looked at him. She wasn't quite in touching distance. "It's car trouble, she said. She's running a little late. You can wait half an hour, can't you?"

He shook his head. Took a sip of tea and a bite of cold toast.

She closed her eyes. Compassion tried and rejected she turned to an emotion she was really good at. Annoyance.

"You'll have to manage. You're an adult, Daniel. I know you've got problems, but..." she shook her head, exasperated. "...I can't do this now. We'll talk tonight."

Except they wouldn't.

She swept out of the kitchen, grabbed the car keys from the table in the hall and slammed the front door behind her.

"I'll be gone by tonight," Daniel said into the silence. He dropped the toast crust onto the plate and stared at his hands. They were shaking.

He washed the breakfast things then dried them methodically, gazing through the condensation-blurred window at the long back garden. A pair of Jays muscled past assorted tits and finches and laid waste to the stale bread and peanuts on the bird table. Their bright colours seemed gaudy, incongruous against the drab olive and earth camouflage of the winter garden.

Daniel dried his hands then held them out so that they were backlit by the sour daylight beyond the window. His hands were always the first to go. But at least he wasn't fading yet. He knew that he would, though. It was only a matter of time.

He sat at the table again, rubbed his eyes, let his breathing slow. He could still smell Helen's perfume. It was something heavy and floral. He didn't like it much, but he was glad of the distraction. He closed his eyes and tried to hold the taste and the smell of it in his mind and at the back of his throat as he sat and waited for his sister.

Twenty minutes later panic bubbled in the pit of Daniel's stomach and rose into his chest. All trace of Helen had gone and Sarah's mobile was still switched off. He put his hands flat on the kitchen table, forcing the tremor out of them. He saw the first traces of the pine's rough grain through his skin and bone.

Ten minutes later, speaking on the phone to his GP's receptionist he said, "I need a home visit. Urgently. And it must be Dr Harland. He knows my...situation."

"That's Mr White, isn't it?" the receptionist said. Pleasant, but wary. "Are you sure it's an emergency, Mr White?"

"Of course I'm sure." He waited, but there was no response. "I'm having a heart attack," he said.

There was a long pause. "We've been through this before, haven't we Mr White?"

"Yes. I'm sorry." He looked at the receiver. It was beige and the plastic shone through his slender fingers. There was a mirror on the wall, a couple of feet away, but he couldn't bring himself to look at it. "But, please. I need help."

"I know you do." Her voice was a curious mixture of kindness and distance, but it was the distance that Daniel felt the most. "I can make you an appointment for this afternoon. But Dr Harland's out, I'm afraid. It would have to be Dr Lassiter."

"That's no good. I can't come out. And anyway it would have to be Harland. I need someone I know. Someone who knows me."

"I'm sorry then. I don't think we can help."

"I know you can't. I don't think anyone can." He broke the connection. He tried his sister's number again, but it was still turned off. Then he dialled another number and as he waited for an answer he looked the watercolour of the Norfolk Broads on the wall and at the occasional traffic that hissed past the frosted glass of the front door. He looked at anything except his hands.

*

"I don't like this," Sarah said again and saw Helen's mouth tighten. They were sitting in the coffee shop at the top of Elm Hill and they each had an untouched Danish pastry and a cup of cappuccino in front of them.

"Tough love, Sarah," Helen said. "It's for his own good. I thought we agreed. We can't keep indulging him."

"He's ill. I feel awful just leaving him on his own. What if he hurts himself?"

Helen stirred her coffee for the third time and pushed an imaginary hair back in place. "He'll be fine. And we'll prove to him that he's fine. That he won't just disappear." She shook her head. "God knows what goes on in that head of his. If we can show him that he's OK perhaps he'll just take his Prozac like everybody else and sort himself out. And we can all get on with our lives."

Sarah looked at her sister-in-law's precisely perfect face and fought the urge to punch it. It was Sarah who sat with Daniel almost every day. Helen's life had sailed on undisturbed. Her career at Norwich Union. Her affair with a senior colleague. Sarah's own marriage had finally expired after a long illness a year ago. She loved her younger brother and didn't begrudge him her time. But he was hardly good company. They were too similar; physically frail, clever but needy, easily hurt. And his current obsession was hard to live with. It was Helen's utter detachment that almost shook Sarah from her meekness.

Helen took a tiny sip of coffee and licked her lips dry. She smiled, although as usual the smile never got close to her eyes. "You all right, Sarah? You were off in a little world of your own for a moment. Just like your brother."

Sarah managed a tight smile in return. She imagined pouring her coffee over Helen's head. "You and Brian," Sarah said, "I hope you can keep that to yourself until Daniel's better. He couldn't take it at the moment. You know that."

"Yes, yes," Helen said. "It can keep. Brian's not keen on telling his wife yet, anyway. Don't look at me like that. You can hardly blame me, Sarah. It's not been much of a marriage this last couple of years. I'm sure you'd rather I didn't go into the details."

"God, no," Sarah said. She stared down at her hands. The eczema rash on her slim fingers was bright red against the white tablecloth.

*

"Son, brother, husband," Daniel said. He was on the telephone to the Samaritans, speaking to a man called Bill.

"That's how you see yourself?" Bill said. Daniel thought Bill's voice was as warm and smooth as melting chocolate. It soothed him. The words didn't matter. Talking to this kind stranger wouldn't change anything, but it helped anyway.

"That's all I am. Well, not even that, actually. My parents are dead, so I'm no longer a son. Brother and husband. I haven't got any friends. Not close enough to count, anyway."

"And you feel, psychologically, that when you're on your own, or more specifically, not in the company of your sister or your wife, that you lose your identity. Metaphorically, you cease to exist."

"Not metaphorically. Physically."

There was a pause. "You know how that sounds."

"I know exactly how it sounds. And I know that no matter how kind and well meaning you are you can't believe me. Neither can my GP, or the police, or the receptionist at Helen's office. I don't blame any of you. But the fact is, in less than half an hour I'll be gone. Physically. As I sit here I'm fading. Becoming less. I can see the seat of the chair that I'm sitting on through my legs. Even my clothes are going. My arm rests on the telephone table and the dark oak veneer is clear in every detail. I can see the ring marks from old coffee cups. There's no pain and as I fade the fear recedes. Detachment is understandable under the circumstances, I suppose. My voice is fading, isn't it?"

"No, Daniel. Your voice is fine."

"I suspect you're just saying that."

"Not at all. Tell me, can you still feel things? The

receiver in your hand. The table beneath your arm."

This time Daniel paused. "Yes. Just about. I'm holding on."

"Why not walk out into the street. Grab the first person you see. Can't they confirm that you exist? Make you real again?"

"If only it was that easy. They'd be strangers. To them I'd be just like a ghost. Anyway, I'm agoraphobic. I haven't been outside since I lost my job nearly a year ago."

"What did you do?"

"Motor insurance. Norwich Union. Same as Helen. It's where we met."

"Did your work give you a sense of identity?"

"God, no. Just the opposite. I think that's where it started. People staring at me. Looking through me." Daniel put a hand across his face. He felt light and faint, and red and black stars pulsed behind his eyes. "God," he said, "it's getting worse."

"Look, Daniel, have you taken anything. An overdose, something like that."

Daniel laughed and to him it sounded as though the laughter came from miles away. "No. Nothing like that. Not even an aspirin. I'm a reformed drunk. I won't even take cough medicine these days. That's why I won't take their bloody anti-depressants. I'm as clean as a whistle, Bill. At least I'll die sober."

"You're not dying, Daniel."

"I beg to differ. I'm becoming less. Less and less." He laughed again, shrilly. "Have you ever seen `Cracker`? With Robbie Coltrane. You know when Billborough got stabbed and when Jimmy jumped off that roof? This is the last statement of a dying man. They both said that. Christ, Bill. My voice is going now, isn't it? I can hardly hear myself."

A pause. "Look, I can get someone round. An ambulance."

"Too late. And it wouldn't help anyway. That's not why I called. I just wanted some company. Thanks for that, Bill. And don't bother trying 1471, it won't work. I'm so tired."

"Daniel?"

"Tell my sister I love her."

"This is stupid. You'll be fine. You're just fainting. It's probably stress, high blood pressure or something. I'll get some help, Daniel. Daniel?"

But the connection was broken.

*

It was mid-afternoon and the first rain was clattering through the near darkness when Helen steered her burgundy Polo into a space a couple of doors down from her terraced house.

"Don't look so worried," she said, "he'll be fine."

Sarah stared through the rain-streaked windscreen and said nothing.

Helen undid her seat belt. "Come on, Sarah. I want to get back to work."

Sarah stirred reluctantly. "I'm afraid he'll hate me. For abandoning him."

Helen snorted. "Daniel couldn't hurt anyone. He hasn't got it in him."

Sarah glanced across at her sister-in-law and thought how typical it was of her to make a compliment sound like an insult.

She stepped into the wet cold air. Her breathing eased. In the confines of the car Helen's heavy, floral perfume had aggravated her asthma.

The house was a three-story Victorian terrace with a bay window and a frosted glass-panelled door. The front of the house was exposed brick and the window frames were stained the colour of teak.

Helen unlocked the front door and pushed it open. Sarah stood on the concrete path a couple of steps behind her.

Helen hesitated on the threshold.

"He's gone," Sarah said.

"Don't be ridiculous," Helen said, and walked into the hallway. She opened the door to the lounge, tossed her handbag onto the nearest armchair and stepped back into the hall. "Close the door, Sarah, you're letting the heat out."

Sarah did as she was told. She felt calm, detached. She noticed that Helen, before she stepped into the kitchen, checked her hair and make-up in the full-length mirror.

Sarah followed Helen towards the kitchen. She hesitated by the telephone, which sat on a small oak unit. The chair next to the unit was at an angle. She stroked the beige plastic receiver and felt nothing.

"Come on, Daniel, stop pissing about," Helen called.

"He's gone," Sarah said.

"Gone where," Helen said. "I locked him in. I've got the only keys. The windows are all still closed, and anyway he hasn't been out of the house since God knows when. No, he's just playing silly buggers. Trying to punish us."

"But there's no sense of him at all," Sarah said, "not even his deodorant or aftershave. Nothing. He's gone, Helen."

"If you say that again I'll…" Helen shook her head angrily, pulled her coat off and threw it over the kitchen table. "Look, we'll search the place. We'll find him. Then you can stay with your precious brother and I can get back to work."

About half an hour later they were back in the kitchen. Helen stood by the kettle, chewing her bottom lip. Sarah sat at the table and stared at her hands. She was still calm, but her eczema was starting to bite. She rubbed her fingers against the table edge.

The kettle boiled. Helen poured hot water roughly into two mugs and slammed the kettle down again. "God help him when I find him," she said.

"You won't find him. Nobody will."

Helen closed her eyes. "Give it a rest, Sarah. You're starting to seriously piss me off."

"I tried redial on the telephone," Sarah said.

Helen looked at her. "And?"

"He phoned the Samaritans."

Helen shrugged. "So? It's not the first time. I think he has them on his frequent user list."

Sarah looked at her sister-in-law as though for the first time. And smiled. The curtains were drawn, the muted fluorescent tube filled the kitchen with a rustic light. Helen looked older, she thought. Smaller, somehow.

"It's a bit sad," Sarah said. "Daniel finding it easier to speak to strangers than to his own wife."

Helen shrugged again and attempted a smile. It wasn't a success. She stood with her back to the sink. It may have been a trick of the light but Sarah was sure she could see the outline of the kettle through Helen's arm.

Family Game

Above the meadow to my left a Kestrel or a Sparrowhawk hovers briefly in the cloudless sky then drops into the long grass as though weighted with lead shot.

I frown, my face pressed against the window. Julie's driving. It's hot outside. The windows in our Sierra Estate are closed and the air-conditioning gushes frigid air across my face and legs. The noise of it makes conversation difficult. Which suits us both.

The meadow has gone now. I wonder if it was a Kestrel or a Sparrowhawk. I can't remember which is bigger. I don't suppose that it matters much to the small wrecked thing at the bottom of its dive.

We take a left turn at the next crossroads and then the next right down a dirt track. The track is rutted and hard as iron. The car shudders and Julie swears and grips the steering wheel harder.

"Nearly there," I say.

Julie grunts.

It is late September but the month long heatwave shows no sign of ending. The fields that trundle close by look drained and tired.

"I said I'd drive," I say.

"I'm fine driving. It's nothing to do with driving. It's this bloody heat."

"Well, it's not hot in here," I say, raising my voice above the roar of the air-conditioning.

"Speak for yourself. You're not six months pregnant, are you?"

There's not much I can say to that so as usual I take refuge in silence.

My sister's house is set in a dozen acres of Norfolk wilderness that is itself engulfed by miles of fens and heaths and brief dense woods.

We approach from the east. The driveway is long and narrow and winds beneath the branches of beech trees. Brittle sunlight angles through the leaves.

Julie wears a blue cotton maternity dress. Her face is

red. Her eyes and mouth are tight with concentration. Her fair hair is pulled back into a pigtail, held in place by a black velvet scrunchy.

"I'm having a drink," Julie says as we pass a vast mottled lawn and approach the shingled parking area at the front of the house. "Some wine with dinner."

"I didn't say anything."

"You don't have to. I know you disapprove."

I close my eyes and say nothing.

"I don't suppose a couple of glasses of wine will hurt your precious baby."

"Our baby," I say slowly, eyes still closed.

She drives past a fountain in the middle of the shingled area and parks next to an ivy-covered retaining wall.

"Can't smoke, can't drink."

"Julie, you've never smoked."

"And as for sex, well…all I can say is it's a wonder the poor little sod ever got conceived in the first place."

"For Christ's sake, don't start that again. It's Karen's birthday. Let's try to be nice, can we? Just for the weekend?"

"Oh, I'm sorry, Paul. I forgot. Mustn't upset your sister. God forbid."

I sigh deeply and push the car door open. The heat is ludicrous. The contrast from the car's frigid interior makes me giddy.

It takes Julie almost a minute to extract herself fully from the driver's seat.

"Thanks for your help," she says. She runs a hand across her forehead, squinting up at the near-white sky. "Fucking hell, it's like an oven out here."

Julie hates my sister's house. I love it. It's over five hundred years old although most of the original building is lost amid extensions, additions, reconstructions. A melody of styles and fads and fashions co-exist here. Three floors, four en-suite bedrooms, a vast staircase that zigzags up from the entrance hall to wide landings on each floor. At one point a turret was added to the eastern edge of the house for no apparent reason. Gargoyles adorn the guttering along the western face. Marble columns sit either side of the oak front door. Stone steps lead down from the door to the drive.

Karen meets us at the bottom step. She's fifty today. A young fifty. I'm nearly twenty years younger. She's tall and willowy. She wears a short white cotton dress. Her legs are slim and brown. She has an elegance inherited from our mother. I don't. Her hair is dark and cut fashionably short. She looks younger when she smiles and she smiles frequently.

She is smiling now, slender arms outstretched.

"Julie, you look wonderful."

"Well, I feel like shit."

"Darling, you're simply glowing. Pregnancy suits you."

I wince. Julie's eyebrows arch. Her face is the colour of boiled ham and sweat cuts dark streaks through her fair hair. "Really?" she says.

"Oh yes. I expect it's a bit wretched in this heat, but I'm sure the worst is over. It's all downhill from here, you'll see."

The women embrace briefly. "That's such a comfort. Remind me, Karen. How many children have you had exactly?"

Karen's smile falters, but only a fraction and only for a moment.

"You get in the shade, love," she says, ushering Julie into the hallway. "Go through to the kitchen. Philip's fixing drinks. He's so looking forward to seeing you."

I bet he is, I think.

Julie waddles into the gloom. Karen gives me a look. "Poor Paul," she says.

She rests her hands on my shoulders and kisses my cheek. Her lips are cool. I smell her perfume. I put a hand on her slim waist.

"Poor Paul indeed," I say. I feel the tightness in my stomach ease.

"You know it's only her hormones, don't you?" she says.

"I'm not so sure," I say. "I think aliens have abducted the real Julie and sent this thing in her place."

She pulls away from me and I let her go reluctantly. She reaches a hand to my face. Her fingers are cool.

"You need a shave," she says.

"I thought I'd try a beard."

Her nose wrinkles. "Oh don't. It won't suit you. You look younger clean shaven. More handsome."

I nod and look down. She wears white sandals with modest heels. Her toenails are painted burgundy.

Karen sighs. "Poor Julie," she says. "She was such a sweet young thing." She pauses. "It's not just the pregnancy, is it?"

I look up at her then my eyes cut away to the heat haze in the distance.

"No. It's not just the pregnancy."

I follow Karen through the hallway. The carpet is crimson and black and feels inches thick. The woodwork in the hallway and the staircase is deep mahogany. There's an unlit open fireplace opposite surrounded with glazed terracotta tiles.

Philip and Julie are in the kitchen, chatting easily. Naturally an Aga dominates one wall. The kitchen is larger than our lounge. There's a breakfast bar in the corner and a pine table that could seat a dozen at a pinch monopolises the far end.

I shake hands with Philip. Reluctantly. His grip is firm and damp and repulsive all at the same time.

"Just chatting up your little lady," he says, "hope you don't mind." He pats Julie's stomach. "Who's a clever girl?" he says.

Julie giggles. The last time I patted her stomach she told me to fuck off. I stare at her and she avoids my gaze.

Philip is tall and broad with a bright ruddy face and sandy hair. His complexion owes much to his malt whisky addiction. He's a Londoner. I try not to hold it against him. He made a small fortune in scrap metal in the seventies and a larger one from recycled building materials a decade later. I could just about forgive his borderline fascism and his obsession with all things Thatcher if he wasn't such an unreconstructed, loud-mouthed twat.

But he is. And my sister married him. Shit happens as they say.

Philip drinks some whisky and clinks his glass against Julie's glass, which is full of ice and a clear liquid.

"I hope that's lemonade," I say. I know how boorish I sound but I can't help myself.

"Of course it's lemonade," Philip booms, aiming a hammy wink at Julie. She winks back and giggles again. She looks at me briefly. "Lemonade," she says, then looks back at Philip.

"A bit early isn't it?" I say.

Philip rolls his eyes. "It's gone four, Paul. Anyway, it's Karen's birthday. We're celebrating, aren't we, Julie?"

She giggles yet again. In agreement. I resist the urge to throttle her. Instead I close my eyes and wish I were somewhere else. Beruit, perhaps.

Then Karen's there, her hand on my arm. "Come on, Paul. Have a beer. I'll get a cold one from the fridge."

I smile my thanks. "And happy birthday," I say. "Your present's in the car. I'll get it later."

"No rush, no rush," she says. She smiles and drinks. Her lips are wet with wine and there's a look of quiet desperation in her eyes.

"Flirt a little more, why don't you?" It's just after five thirty and Julie and I are unpacking in our room.

"Well, at least he notices me."

"Believe me, with Philip, that's not a compliment."

"He's always liked me. At least he's got some life in him."

I slip my boxer shorts and clean socks into a drawer in a small oak dresser. It smells faintly of lavender.

"It's nice being fancied again. I've forgotten what it's like. When did you last touch me, Paul? My memory's not that good."

I keep my back to her. "I'm scared of hurting the baby. You know that."

"And what was your excuse before the baby, Paul?"

"I got you pregnant, didn't I? Must have done something right."

"That's a matter of opinion."

I turn and look at her. Her mouth is set in a thin hard line that I've come to recognise and loathe. I wonder where the real Julie is. I'm sure she's in there somewhere. I hope she is.

She turns and folds her navy maternity knickers neatly and puts them away. "Anyway, I can't compete with the lovely Karen, can I?"

I stop what I'm doing. "What's that supposed to mean?"

"The way you look at her."

"She's my sister."

"Precisely."

"What does that mean?"

"You work it out."

I turn back to the dresser. I open a drawer, close it again. "You've gone too far this time," I say.

"If you blame it on my hormones I'll hit you, I swear I will," Julie says.

For a moment I think of hitting her. I consider it in some detail. Then a voice floats up from the landing below. Philip. Who else. "Must be for you," I say. My voice seems flat and stiff.

Julie's face changes. She opens the door and shouts down. "Coming, Philip."

Downstairs I say, "Shooting rabbits? You don't like guns. You don't like rabbits. This makes no sense."

Julie stands with her arms folded and stares past my left shoulder. Philip breezes into the hallway. Despite the heat he wears a Barbour jacket. He carries a broken twelve bore over one arm.

"Just bagging some bunnies, Paul. You're welcome to join us." He sees the look on my face. "Got to be done, mate. Little bastards'll overrun us otherwise."

"But Julie hates guns. Hates shooting things."

Philip shrugs. "Well now she wants to give it a try. No big deal. Perhaps it's her hormones."

Julie giggles.

"Let them go," Karen says. She sits on the stairs behind us. Her legs are crossed. Her chin rests in one hand. She has a glass of pale wine in the other.

Philip turns. "Sure you don't want to come, love?" There's a sneer in his voice that I don't like at all.

"You go on," she says, not looking at him. "Just keep the poor little things away from me."

There's an interior door, a small porch, then the large oak front door. Philip and Julie go through them into the early evening heat. Some of it seeps into the shaded hall. Philip's voice and Julie's giggles recede.

We sigh simultaneously.

I sit next to Karen on the stairs. "How the hell did you end up with him?" I've asked the question before and she gives the usual answer.

"He was quite a catch back in '75. Big hair, big lapels. Bundles of one pound notes in his back pocket. Enough to turn a girl's head."

"Sounds a lot easier in those days. I think I was born too late."

We look at each other briefly and say nothing. The silence is comfortable.

Then Karen says, "I like it when Philip goes shooting." She pauses and I look at her. As if on cue both barrels of the shotgun echo in the distance. "There's always a chance he'll blow his fucking head off."

Her face shows no expression. But I catch the sparkle in her green eyes and start to laugh. We hear the gun again, bruising the quiet of the Norfolk afternoon.

Before dinner I shave carefully and put on some after-shave and a clean shirt. Sweat gathers immediately on my back and beneath my arms. Julie wears make-up for the first time in months.

A beautifully set rectangular oak table dominates the dining room. We eat by candlelight. Karen serves venison and roast vegetables. Philip drinks whisky with his meal. Karen and I drink white wine; Julie keeps her glass topped up from a bottle of Californian red.

I eat slowly and watch Julie drink. Eventually I smile and say softly, "Don't you think you've had enough, love?"

She looks at me and shakes her head. Her made-up face shines in the candlelight. I realise she repulses me.

"Let her be," Philip says, smiling. "Got to enjoy yourself sometime, haven't you Julie? Let your hair down."

She looks at Philip. "That's right," she says. She simpers a little, but at least she doesn't giggle.

I feel I can't leave it alone. "But the baby..."

"Oh, fuck the baby," Julie says, turning to me, her face changing again. Too much mascara, I think. And the lipstick's all wrong. "I should have tried gin and a coat hanger months ago."

There's a small, charged silence. Even Philip looks embarrassed. Then Karen says, "More vegetables, Paul?"

I take some parsnips and honey glazed carrots. Her green eyes meet mine. Her make-up is minimal, I notice. A touch of lip gloss, a little blusher. Her nails are painted the colour of dark wine. She wears an ivory silk blouse and a long black skirt.

Somehow we make it to dessert. Then Philip asks me about work and my heart sinks.

"It's fine thanks," I say.

"The cut and thrust of local government. Heady stuff."

I smile stiffly.

"Pity about that promotion. Julie told me you didn't get it."

"Perhaps next year."

"Perhaps."

He leaves a small silence and like a fool I fill it. "I know it doesn't sound much. Working for the council. But it does matter. Local democracy and all that. Working for the people."

"Absolutely," Philip says. "Vital stuff. I'm sure you're a crucial, if rather small cog in a well-oiled machine. God knows what we'd do without you."

Sweat beads his forehead. It's probably seventy-percent proof. Julie watches, fascinated, a spoonful of toffee roulade halfway to her lips. Karen seems somewhere else entirely. I can't say I blame her.

Philip is now primed for his obligatory self made man speech and he doesn't disappoint. I tune him out. I drink some wine and wait for him to come up for air.

Later, still at the table, we drink coffee and brandy. Philip smokes a cigar. "Could've had a proper party," he says, waving his arms expansively. He is, I realise, extremely pissed. "No expense spared, that's what I said. Could've had my mates round. They'd have livened the place up. But no. The birthday girl wants family, the birthday girl gets family." He smiles unpleasantly.

"The only family I have left," Karen says softly, gazing into her coffee.

"Apart from me," Philip says.

Karen ignores him. She fingers her necklace. "Thanks for this, you two. It's beautiful. Did you choose it, Julie?"

Julie sips her brandy. "No. I left it to Paul. Same as I leave most things to Paul. Like responsibility for contraception, for instance."

"More coffee," Karen says quickly, but it's too late.

"What's this?" Philip says. "Bit of a slip up, was it Paul? Careless old boy. Very careless. Slipshod. Pretty much what I'd expect from the council, come to think of it."

I feel my face redden. "I really don't think..."

"Oh, forget it, old boy. No need to apologise. Anyway, it suits you, Julie, it really does. You look wonderful. Wonderful. I've always had a thing about pregnant women." He turns to Karen. "Haven't I, love?"

Karen stares at the table. She puts her hands to her mouth. Then she stands, puts the coffee things methodically onto the tray and leaves the room.

Fifteen years ago she had two miscarriages in eighteen months.

Philip shrugs and smiles at Julie. I imagine sliding the barrels of his shotgun into his mouth and pulling both triggers.

Later that night I lay on my back in bed with my hands linked behind my head and listen to Julie's snores. She lays on her side with her back to me. There's about six inches between us. It may as well be a mile. Make that ten miles. A hundred.

I gaze up at the ceiling. The curtains and window are open. Moonlight angles in. The air is stale and hot. As though it's been recycled too often. The wilderness surrounding my sister's house is utterly quiet.

The volume of Julie's snoring increases and the tone deepens.

Ten years ago, in late November, we rented a cottage close to Derwent Water. It pissed down all weekend. We made love almost continuously. We touched and talked and laughed. The details have gone; the clothes she wore, what we talked about. But I remember her smile and how her eyes shone. I remember my mild astonishment that I could be the reason for another person's happiness.

It's been downhill ever since. Perhaps it always is. With almost geological slowness we've inched apart, minute by minute, hour by hour, until, years later, there's a fucking great chasm between us that neither of us has the first idea how to bridge. Or if we even want to.

And then there's the baby. I'm sure it's a boy. May as well call the poor little sod Damien and tattoo 666 on his arse. These things happen. Nobodies fault. Careless, though. Bloody careless. I close my eyes. Sleep still seems an age away.

I wake suddenly. I'm lying on my stomach, my face buried in the pillow. The pillow is wet. I roll onto my back. I grab the alarm clock and hold it close to my face. Just after three.

Something's missing. No snores. I fling out an arm. Julie's side of the bed is empty. I'm surprised that I care. She's probably in the bathroom so I wait a while and wonder what woke me.

Ten minutes later I pad down the three flights of stairs. The carpet is soft beneath my bare feet. I wear only a pair of blue cotton pyjama trousers. The stairs creak faintly under my weight.

In the hallway I hear a sound from the kitchen. Someone giggling. When I push the door open the brightness of the light dazzles me. Julie and Philip are standing by the breakfast bar. They move apart from one another almost comically. Philip has on a white T-shirt and grey flannel shorts. Julie wears just her pink maternity nightdress. It occurs to me suddenly how large her breasts have become.

"Couldn't sleep," Philip says. "Fancied a drink." He holds up the tumbler in his right hand. "Want one?"

"No," I say.

"Thought I heard a noise," Julie says. "Thought I'd better have a look. Didn't know it was Philip, did I?" She sees me looking at the empty glass on the breakfast bar, inches from her hand. "Needed something to calm my nerves," she says.

"Purely medicinal," I say.

"That's right."

I cock my head to one side. "What's the problem? Why do you both look so guilty?"

"We don't," Philip says.

"Yes you do. You're both blushing like hell." At least I think they are. It's hard to tell with their complexions. "What's up, Philip? Don't tell me you were going to pin her over the kitchen table."

Julie gasps. Philip says, "Don't be so crude, man. You've got it all wrong."

"Whatever," I say. "I'm going to bed. Goodnight." I close the door behind me. I feel a strange elation as I climb the stairs. A bit like a sugar high. I know I'll pay for it later.

I'm still awake when Julie comes to bed. She lies on her side, her back to me, without speaking. I turn towards her. I realise with some surprise that I have an erection. The tip of it brushes Julie's nightdress. I move a fraction closer.

"What are you doing?" Julie says.

I say nothing, just move closer still, so that I'm pressed up against her buttocks. She wriggles away and I follow her.

"I thought you wanted it," I say. I try to push the head of my cock between her thighs.

"Don't flatter yourself," she says. She pushes me back and sits on the edge of the bed. "If you're that desperate go and have a wank."

I roll out of bed. Clumsily. My forlorn erection gets snagged in the sheets. My face is hot. I can think of nothing to say so I follow my cock out of the bedroom door.

Downstairs again I go to the kitchen. It's dark and empty. I drink some water. My face and chest are wet with sweat. In one of the living rooms I open the French doors and step onto a small paved area that leads to an expanse of lawn. The concrete is cold beneath my feet. In the moonlight I can see as far as the first huddle of trees. Beyond that shadows lurk. The air is thick and still and difficult to breathe.

I smell Karen before I hear her. Perfume and shampoo. I

turn and she pauses a couple of feet from me. She should look older with her make-up gone but she doesn't. Her face is pale. She wears a knee-length black silk nightdress. Her arms and bare shoulders are brown but her skin turns white as it dips towards her breasts.

"Paul?" she says. Tentatively.

I don't trust myself to speak. My throat feels thick, my eyes hot.

I put my hands to my face. "Oh, shit," I say.

I hear the rustle of her nightdress as she moves towards me. She takes me in her arms. My hands drop to her waist and I pull her closer. Her hands stroke the back of my neck. My face is by her throat. I can feel her pulse there, close to my lips. I smell her perfume and her clean hair.

I feel my erection again, pressing hard against her flat stomach. For a moment neither of us moves. Then she withdraws a fraction and so do I. I pull my face from her neck.

"God, I'm sorry," I say.

She smiles at me but her cheeks are red. "Don't be silly," she says.

I realise there are tears on my face and on hers too.

Her hands are on my shoulders now. She's close enough that I can feel her breath. My erection still strains towards her. Neither of us looks down.

It feels as though my nerves are on the outside of my skin. Her fingertips move a fraction and my senses scream. My heart hammers in my chest. I need to come. The merest touch will do it. God forgive me but I want her fingers to drop to my chest and then lower still.

My hands are on her hips and her skin is hot beneath the silk. I try, minutely, to pull her towards me, to give her the slightest excuse to hold me again. But she resists. I look into her eyes and what I see there breaks my heart. She takes her hands from my shoulders and my arms drop to my sides. She leans forward from a safe distance and kisses my cheek. It's a chaste kiss. A sister's kiss. But it burns anyway.

Then she's gone.

I stand for a while in the darkness and let the decades of shame and guilt and self-disgust have their way with me.

A little later I sit in the kitchen, smoking. I gave up four years ago but what the hell. I hear a noise outside the kitchen door. I hope that it's Karen. Or Julie at a pinch. But my luck holds and it's Philip.

"You again," he says.

"Apparently."

He fetches his tumbler from the draining board and half fills it with whisky. He looks at me. "Have you been nicking my fags?"

"Didn't think you'd mind. Considering you tried to shag my wife."

"Don't start that again."

"Don't get me wrong. You can fuck her until her teeth rattle for all I care."

He swallows some whisky, then takes a cigarette from the packet of Silk Cut and lights it. "It's Karen you should be worried about."

"Why?"

"She's lying upstairs crying her eyes out. Have you upset her?"

"Don't be a prat. It's probably you."

He opens the kitchen door and flicks ash into the darkness. "I can't hurt her anymore, Paul. You know that."

"You still have a fucking good try, don't you?"

"It's you, Paul. Not me. She's always been more than a sister to you, hasn't she?"

I look up at him sharply. "What's that supposed to mean?"

"Easy tiger," he says. "How old were you when your mum died? Five? Six? And your dad was long gone. She brought you up, didn't she? Made sacrifices for you. The state you and Julie are in, it breaks her heart."

He drains his glass and puts it back in the sink. He goes back to the doorway and blows smoke into the night.

"You broke her heart, you bastard," I say, "and her spirit."

He still has his back to me. He laughs. "I still love her, really. It's just a game we play. You'll understand when you grow up."

I stand quietly. On the floor, next to the Aga, there's a black wrought iron doorstop in the shape of a Golden Retriever. I pick it up. It's heavy. Philip finishes his cigarette and flicks it into the night. I watch its tip cartwheel through the darkness. I move up to him and bring the doorstop down onto the back of his head. He grunts and falls forward. He stays on his knees for a moment, wavering. His breathing is rapid, irregular. I hit him again. Boneless, he crumples forward.

His scalp is awash with blood, dark in the moonlight, flooding his fair hair. I'm not sure if he's breathing.

I put the doorstop on the concrete outside. I step backwards into the kitchen, close the door, lock it.

I stand in silence, straining for signs of movement from upstairs. Absurdly, I half expect to hear sirens in the distance and then the hiss of displaced gravel as the police cars pull up in the drive.

I sit at the kitchen table for half an hour, drinking Philip's whisky. The house is still quiet. I pad into the hallway and take our car keys from the telephone table. I go out through the front door, lock it from the outside, push the keys through the letterbox.

The Sierra's pedals feel strange under my bare feet. I start the engine. The seat belt is cold against my chest. As the headlights sweep across the meadow rabbits scatter for the long grass.

It's four thirty in the morning and owls are hunting beneath a gibbous moon.

Something About Her

The last time I saw my brother he shot me a grin and a wink. He punched my shoulder and told me he loved me. I dropped my head, embarrassed, looked at my feet. When I looked up again he'd gone.

Three years later Jan and I are on Cromer beach, standing at the water's edge. The sea is wild in the cold wind. Green water fizzes around my Doc Marten's and Jan's black knee length boots. Her arm is linked in mine. Her cheeks are beaten bright pink by the wind, her black hair tugged in stiff ribbons behind her.

She tries to speak and the words tumble away from me. Grinning, she pulls me from the sea's edge. With the wind at our back we can speak again. My face feels as though it's been savaged numb. I love it though. The thought of how snug we'll be later; in the lamplight, curtains drawn, fire on, curled together on our old sofa.

Low clouds scud by, wringing the daylight out, fast-forwarding to dusk. The light is metallic, almost monochrome. It should be bleak, God knows it's trying to be. But it isn't.

Eight years married, still holding hands, still sharing walks on winter beaches. Corny, or what?

"What were you trying to say? A minute ago?" I still have to shout to make myself heard.

She shrugs and smiles. "Can't remember. Nothing important." Our faces are close. She smells of salt. I kiss her hair. She tastes of salt too.

The gale at our back urges us towards the concrete steps that lead to the promenade. As though it's guarding the sea. Helping it keep its secrets. I glance backwards and get a face full of frigid air. I look at the sea again and wonder what it isn't saying.

We take refuge in a second-hand bookshop, tucked away in a back street. Jan browses amongst the crime and horror.

"Danny brought me here," I say. I look around, trying to find a sense of him.

"I know," she says, "you told me before." There's no reproach in her voice and she smiles as she speaks. I talk about Danny often. So does she. It could be indulgence on her part, but I know it's more than that. She loved Danny too. I don't blame her for it. Everybody loved Danny.

And she doesn't know that I know. That's fine, too.

It's January but one of the arcades is open. "It used to be all Operation Wolf and Rainbow Islands when Danny and I were here," I say. I look around at the cockpits and the flight simulators and the football game where you actually kick a ball and my shoulders slump. "I feel old all of a sudden."

"Time to face facts, Grandad," Jan says. Her grey eyes sparkle. "Receding hairline, memory loss. Lack of sex drive. All the classic signs."

"Well, two out of three's not bad."

Jan smiles. "That rather depends which two, doesn't it?"

There are perhaps half a dozen of us in the arcade. The sound of the machines is desultory. One of sulky neglect. The wind howls in jealously through the open front.

Jan undoes her coat and loosens her scarf and beats me five-two at air hockey. I get a score of thirty on "Whack-A-Croc", which I think is pretty respectable until a kid of perhaps ten racks up eighty-seven while expending most of his energy and concentration on extracting something large and irksome from his nose with his free hand.

"Can't be good at everything," I sigh.

Jan puts her hand on my arm and rests her head briefly on my shoulder.

Later we drink tea in a café that's quaint if your idea of quaint is shabby and rundown.

"Danny was nineteen when he brought me here. Two years after mum left. God knows where he got the money from." We exchange a glance. We both know very well where he got the money but neither of us will ever say it. "It was the end of the season. Played football on the beach. He bought me an ice cream from the kiosk next to the arcade. Strawberry and vanilla. We went to Yarmouth, too. The Pleasurebeach. He went on all the rides with me. I know he hated it. Felt like a prat, he said. But he did it anyway. For me." I blink suddenly and look down. My eyes are hot. "Where the fuck is he, Jan?"

She puts her hands on mine. She wears black woollen

66

gloves but I can feel the heat of her fingers through them. At least I think I can. Her grey eyes hold mine. I see warmth there, and compassion. Her own hurt is tucked away in a corner, just out of my sight.

*

On the first anniversary of Danny's disappearance I found Jan sitting on the edge of our bed, her head in her hands. It was dark outside and the curtains were drawn. The bedside lamp filled the room with buttery light.

"He's dead, isn't he?" she said. Her voice was small, the words muffled by her fingers. She looked up at me. Her eyes were red, her cheeks bright with tears. I stood awkwardly, hands in pockets, shoulders hunched.

"No. Don't even think it. He's not dead. He wouldn't do that to me. To us." It was a lie, of course. His bank account remained untouched. He'd paid the rent on his flat six months in advance. The police had shrugged their shoulders. Said he was an adult, no crime had been committed. There was nothing they could do. But the look in the Duty Sergeant's eyes had matched my own. I'd always believed I could feel if Danny was still alive and at that moment I felt nothing at all.

"I'm sorry, Tom," she said, turning her face away from me again. It looked pale and lost, hardly Jan's face at all.

I sat next to her on the bed. Her hair was cut short then and I kissed her neck. She wore a pink lambs wool sweater with purple petals embroidered on the sleeve and a long pleated skirt.

She turned to me, opening up like a flower. We made love on top of the quilt, the tears still wet on her face, her skirt pulled roughly above her hips. Heat came off her in waves and her kisses were dry. Her eyes were open and staring but I knew it wasn't my face she saw above her. As she came she turned her head to one side and bit her lip. I think she was scared she'd cry out the wrong name.

*

The drive home from Cromer begins well enough. It's dark outside now but we're snug inside our old Astra. We turn the heater up and listen to Radiohead and The B-52's on the tape player. Sing along to Creep and Love Shack.

The country roads are almost empty. The headlights scissor the darkness, picking out the road-kill. Rabbits, hedgehogs, a couple of pheasants.

And the mood changes. The tape ends and the radio kicks in. A song by Annie Lennox comes on and Jan looks stiffly out of her window at the inky fields and the blurred ragged hedgerows.

"What?" I say.

"Do you remember this?" She pauses and listens to the song. "Broken Glass."

I shrug.

"You hated it. I loved it, though. So did Danny. He bought me the single."

"Did he?"

She looks straight into the darkness, her hands folded in front of her.

"Who was she, Tom?"

I don't answer. I pretend I don't understand. Pretend she hasn't asked me the same question a dozen times before.

"Who was Danny meeting that day, Tom. What was her name?"

I know she's looking at me but I stare ahead at the cold dark road.

"I've told you, love. Over and over." I speak quietly but I can't keep the edge of despair from my voice. "I don't know who she was."

She doesn't answer. She turns the radio off. We sit in silence until we hit the outskirts of Norwich.

*

The last day I saw Danny was the Saturday before Christmas and the sun was low in a clear sky and the wind was from the north and had an edge to it. We walked together to the bus stop on St Stephens, struggling through the crowds of Christmas shoppers.

"Who is she, Danny?" I said. "You tell me everything. I thought we had a deal. I get my kicks vicariously, through you. The ultimate safe sex."

Danny laughed. "Not this time, mate. This one's special."

"Shit, that's not wedding bells I can hear, is it?"

"Hardly." He glanced at me with an expression of uncharacteristic coyness. He started to say something, then changed his mind. He looked good, though. Freshly pressed Chinos, best leather jacket, black cable knit sweater. He'd shaved, too, and had his dark hair cut and swept back.

"Come on, Danny. You're holding something back. Tell your little brother all about it. You'll feel so much better."

"Yeah, right. It's nothing. There's just something about her, that's all. She's different."

"Sounds suspiciously like love to me, mate."

"Bollocks," Danny said, accidentally elbowing a middle-aged

68

lady, wearing a bright red coat, in the ribs. She scowled at him briefly but he smiled at her and she melted immediately and smiled back.

"Still got a way with ladies of a certain age, I see."

"Any age," Danny said, "You know that, Tom."

A few minutes later I said, "Right, I'm popping into Marks and Sparks, see what I can get Jan for Christmas. Have a good time, Danny. Be good."

He hesitated, again on the verge of speaking. He tilted his head to one side and aimed a shy smile in my direction.

"Look, Tom, give Jan my love, won't you?"

"Sure. But why? You can do it yourself tomorrow."

"Yeah. That's right."

"What's up, Danny? You're starting to worry me."

"Nothing. Nothing." He moved out of the way of a young woman with a pushchair. "I want to give you something. I shouldn't. But I think I will."

He handed me a crumpled piece of paper. On it were a name and telephone number. I looked at him, puzzled. "Why do I need this? And what's the big deal?" I looked at the paper. "Della. You could've given me her name ages ago."

"You won't need it. And look, this is our secret, right?"

"Secret?"

His face was red. "Yeah. Like I said, she's special. It's hard to explain."

"I think you'd better try. She married or something?"

"Nothing like that. I'll buy you a pint tomorrow. We'll talk about it then." He grinned and winked at me. He punched my shoulder lightly and said, "I love you, Tom."

I blushed and looked at my feet. When I looked up he was lost amongst the Christmas shoppers.

*

The piece of paper is in a ball in my jeans pocket where it burns like phosphorous. The paper is worn, the ink faded, but the words and numbers are still readable. I've memorised them, anyway. I've never used them, though. I don't know why. They haunt me constantly, drag me from my sleep in the early hours and taunt me. I refuse to recognise my fear.

I've kept Danny's secret. It rots inside me.

At home, her hair still wild from the beach, Jan stands by the cooker, heating milk for hot chocolate. I put my hand on her waist. She doesn't pull away but she doesn't yield to me either. I eat a digestive and tease the tangles from her hair.

Later, in the living room, just after midnight, the telephone rings. It rings on and on. Jan and I look at it, and then at each other.

Bloody David Irving

It was the Nine O'Clock News that started it. Out of a clear blue sky, as they say.

We were curled together on the sofa in the living room of my flat in the city centre. Sarah leant her head on my shoulder. Her hair, damp from the shower, smelt of peaches. She wore lemon-coloured cotton pyjamas that buttoned down the front. We'd been inseparable for three months. My mum said it was as though we'd been joined at the hip. She was smiling though. I was her only child, I was the wrong side of thirty and she saw her chance of grandchildren receding with every year.

Sarah wriggled against me. Her breath was warm on my cheek. I felt the first stirrings of yet another erection. "Christ," she said, "aren't you worn out yet?"

"Apparently not," I said.

"I just want to watch the news, then you can fuck me again."

"Elegantly put."

"Oh, it had better be, my dear. It had better be." She kissed me lightly on the mouth. For the last time, as it turned out.

For the past three months we had immersed ourselves in each other. All that mattered was the taste of her lips and of her neck, the texture of her skin and the warmth of her flat stomach beneath the palm of my hand.

Ironic really. I've never believed in all that soul mate shit. I liked the independence of being single. I'd seen friend after friend marry and regret it. Usually sooner rather than later. They changed as well. A look came into their eyes. A distance. A sense of regret. It wasn't for me. I didn't think it would ever be for me.

But what the hell did I know?

*

We met on a sticky Wednesday afternoon in the middle of August at the services on the southbound stretch of the M11, just off the M25. I sat in a plastic chair at a plastic table and drank coffee that tasted like no coffee I'd tasted before.

I was on my way home from a meeting in Bristol. I was hot and dog-tired. I could feel the sweat in my hair and the deodorant that I'd sleepily applied at four o'clock that morning was now fighting a losing battle.

I scarcely noticed her when she sat opposite me. Her choice of seat seemed odd, I suppose, given the acreage of empty Formica between the self-service counter and us.

She put a cup of coffee and a wilted sandwich on the table and pointed at the chair. "D'you mind?" she said.

"Be my guest."

She was youngish, slimmish, with crimped blond hair and blue eyes. There was a brief spray of freckles across the bridge of her snub nose. She was lightly tanned. She had a nice mouth and when she smiled her teeth were white and even.

"I'm Sarah," she said, extending her hand.

"Tim," I said, taking it. Her hand was cool and I was aware how limp and moist mine must have felt by comparison.

She sipped her coffee. "God, that's shite," she said.

"Literally, I should imagine," I said.

She smiled again. "Look, I'm trying to hitch to Norwich. I've got a cousin there. I've been staying with a friend in Nottingham. I found a lorry driver who'd take me this far, which was great, but he spent more time looking at my tits than at the road."

I found it hard to blame him. She wore a low cut caramel-coloured t-shirt and a short denim skirt.

"Well, I live in Norwich, but..."

"Oh, thanks Tim. You're a star. A real lifesaver. My cousin lives in Barrett Street. D'you know it? But anywhere in the city centre's fine, obviously. I've got a little cash. Petrol money."

"I'm on expenses."

"That's cool. I'm going to freshen up. Don't run away."

God help me, I didn't.

I'm a dull man. Even my friends say so, with some justification. I think they'd also say I'm pleasant enough and dependable. But dull.

The journey home took two hours and in that time I changed. Something happened between Sarah and I. I know now that I was chosen. Manipulated. Used. But there was a chemistry between us. I genuinely believe that. I have to.

We chatted blandly enough for a while. I found out she was an art student and that she was between boyfriends. She laughed when I asked about career plans. She had no idea what tomorrow held, she said, let alone next year.

"What about you?" she said. "Married? Engaged?"

"Neither. I'm a bachelor gay," I said, then blushed at my choice of words.

She arched her eyebrows and I laughed. "Not literally," I said, "although I think my mum had her doubts for a while a few years back. Wanted to know when I was going to meet a nice girl and settle down." I shrugged. "I'm not interested, to be honest."

"Never been close?"

"Not really. There was a girl about a year ago, but it fizzled out. Didn't bother me much."

"A year ago? And nobody since?"

"No."

"Shit. I bet you've got a helluva right wrist."

"You speak your mind, Sarah. Don't hold back."

She laughed a deep, throaty laugh that made me look at her then made me laugh too.

"It's no big deal," I said. "Sex and all that. I can take it or leave it."

"You don't know what you're missing, mate."

"I'll take your word for it," I said.

She started to say something, then stopped. She put her hand to her mouth, chuckled softly and stared out of the window.

We sped towards Norfolk's uncompromising flatness. I'm thirty-three years old and I've had two serious relationships. Sarah coaxed this from me gently, then spoiled it a little by laughing hard.

"Nothing wrong with that," I said.

"For a monk."

"We're not all obsessed with sex, you know. All right, it's your turn to confess."

Five minutes later she was still reeling off names and I really wished I hadn't asked. It was like that scene in "Four Weddings" when Andi McDowell answers a similar question from Hugh Grant.

"Christ," I said, "I don't know what's more impressive, your stamina or your memory."

"Jealous."

"Not at all. Underneath all that bluster I don't think you're any happier than I am."

She paused a moment and looked away. "I didn't say I was." She glanced back at me. "Actually, there's more than that. I didn't always get a name."

"Didn't?"

"I've been easing off a little lately. Probably a passing phase. Like soft drugs."

She looked wistful for a moment and her smile, when it came, was not convincing.

"Why am I telling you this?"

"Dunno," I said. "I must have a face you can trust."

"Wouldn't have hitched a lift with you otherwise."

"Not that you gave me much choice."

She tilted her head to one side as she looked at me. "I'm your first hitcher, aren't I?"

"Of course. Mother warned me about girls like you."

"I bet she did."

As we bypassed Thetford the clouds were growing thicker and inching lower. Sarah pulled a bottle of mineral water from her bag and took a long swallow. Some of the water spilled onto her chin and throat. Giggling, she wiped her face and neck. She offered me the bottle. I shook my head.

"So what were their names, then?" she said.

"Who?"

"Your girlfriends. All two of them."

"Helen and Isabel."

She took another pull from the bottle, then tossed it back into the canvas bag that nestled between her brown legs. "Who was the better lover?"

"Christ. I don't know. I wasn't keeping score. Bet you did, though."

"Of course. I'll run through all my ratings if you like."

"No," I said quickly, "that won't be necessary."

"How long did it take you, then? To get them into bed. I bet it was at least a month."

"You're a bad girl, Sarah."

"I'm just inquisitive. Come on. You're blushing. It must have been longer."

"If you must know, it was a month before I even kissed Helen properly. I think with Isabel it was longer than that."

"Bloody hell."

"Mr. Impulsive, that's me."

She shook her head. "Bloody hell," she said again.

"I just like to be sure of myself, that's all. Perhaps I am a little conservative. With a small 'c' of course."

"Just a little," she said.

She fidgeted in her seat, then she yawned and stretched,

arms above her head, back arching like a cat's. I found myself wondering if she purred if you touched her right.

Then she shivered prettily. "Turn the air-conditioning down, Tim. It's chilly in here. Look, my nipples are hard."

"You can't help yourself, can you?" I said, but I did as she asked.

"Rather be too hot than too cold," she said.

Just like a cat, I thought.

Without the air-conditioning the humidity of the day outside soon found it's way inside the car.

I wiped the sweat from my face. "You honestly prefer it like this?" I said. "I feel as though I'm being suffocated by a wet, warm blanket. And I'm sure I stink."

"Pheromones, Tim. Sexy as hell."

"Sexy? I smell like a tramp and you reckon it's sexy."

"Joke, Tim. You don't smell at all. Mind you, it's hard to tell from here." She leant towards the driver's seat and pretended to sniff my arm and neck. I felt her breath and caught a trace of her scent. "No, you're fine," she said.

"Oh, good," I said, glancing across at her. Her blond hair was stained dark with sweat, her face and throat wet with it. I wanted to wipe her face dry, to brush her hair from her eyes.

I looked back at the road. "Oh, shit," I said.

"What?"

"Nothing," I said.

We were close to Norwich now and it was raining, thick, heavy drops attacking the windscreen.

"Can I please open a window," I said. "I'm suffocating here."

She'd reclined her seat a little and she lay back, eyes half closed, lips slightly parted. "No," she said. "This is good. It's like a sauna."

"And that's a good thing, is it?" I looked at her. She was smiling languidly. More and more I found myself stealing glances and she kept meeting them.

As we approached Norwich I found I was driving more slowly. Ten miles an hour under the speed limit instead of five miles an hour over. I didn't know why.

"D'you like this, Tim?" Sarah said, after a comfortable silence.

I was miles away. "What?" I said, turning towards her.

She had lifted the bottom of her t-shirt, exposing a strip of flat, brown stomach. I felt something twist in my chest. Perhaps it was indigestion.

"This," she said, fingering the small silver ring that pierced her navel.

"Lovely," I said. "I'm sure your mother's very proud."

"Grumpy sod," she said, pulling her t-shirt down. I regretted my sharpness. "I think it's great. I'm going to have the next one through my.."

"Yes, yes. Too much detail."

"I was going to say nose."

"Oh."

"You really are screwed up, aren't you?"

After a moment I said, "Yes, I suppose I am."

"Why?"

I shrugged. "I don't know. I've always felt more of an observer than a participant. In life, I mean. Ever since I was a kid. I don't know why."

"Do you feel detached? Apart from everyone, everything?"

"Yes. That's it. That's it exactly."

"Me too."

"You?"

She nodded.

"You hide it well."

She said nothing. It felt warmer still in the car, the air closer, thicker.

"I've grown to like it," I said. "Or, at least that's what I've convinced myself. It's easier if nothing touches you. Can't get hurt." I started to say something else, stopped, then started again. "Even making love, even with Helen and Isabel, who I cared about, or at least I thought I did, even with them it was as though I wasn't really there. I may as well have been sitting across the room, watching."

"Kinky."

"I may as well have been reading a book for all it meant to me." I glanced across at her. She was looking hard at my face. "Do you know what I mean?"

"Yes," she said softly. Her hand slid across, rubbed my arm, the top of my leg. "I know just what you mean."

Much later I knew she'd been playing me like a fish, reeling me in. But then I believed her. Who the hell wouldn't? She was so good I think she believed herself.

"Where does your cousin live? You said earlier, but I've forgotten."

She didn't answer for a moment, then she said, "Does it matter?"

"I don't know," I said. "I don't know, Sarah." It was true. I didn't know what I thought or felt. My voice seemed thick, scarcely my voice at all.

"We'll go to yours, shall we?" Her eyes were wide open, the pupils dilated. "Shall we, Tim?"

"Yes," I said. "God, yes."

The drive home took about ten minutes but it seemed longer. I drove too quickly. We didn't speak.

I parked badly. At the door of my flat I struggled with the door key and she laid her hand on my bare forearm. It felt like an electric shock. We stumbled inside. We were kissing before the door closed. Our teeth clashed but it didn't matter. I tasted the sweat on her neck. She tugged at my shirt and at the waist of my trousers. I pressed against her, pulling her skirt up, my hands on her thighs.

I was almost inside her before we reached the sofa. She thrust back at me, murmuring my name over and over like a mantra. I felt her breath on my neck. There was no detachment now.

We came together; at least I think we did. Looking back, knowing what I know now, I still can't bring myself to believe that she was acting then. The last ten minutes in the car, the first five minutes in my flat, if nothing else was real I have to believe that they were. I can't afford to believe anything else.

She never mentioned her cousin again. She stayed for three months, of which I remember little. Except the sex, and even that's a bit of a blur. Given time my sense of detachment has kicked in again and it's as though it all happened to somebody else.

My work suffered, although I didn't realise this until about six months later. At the time I thought I had everything under control. I took a few sick days, the odd day's holiday at short notice. I suppose I was scruffier than usual and I was late two or three times a week, something unheard of before. It didn't seem to matter. When I was apart from Sarah I counted the hours until we were together again.

Pathetic, I know, but true.

When I was at work she had the run of the flat. Sometimes she cooked for us both, sometimes she didn't. Food didn't seem to matter either. Around the middle of September I remembered that she was an art student and asked her when she was going back to college. She shrugged and said she was taking a year out. She wouldn't speak about her past at all, or her future for that matter. Looking back, most of our conversations seemed to have the clarity and permanence of smoke.

And then there was the sex. I was vulnerable and naïve. Sarah was neither. I'd never experienced anything approaching the intensity of what she offered. I was a rabbit caught in her headlights. Once, visiting my mother, Sarah fellated me on the sofa in the living room while my mother spoke on the telephone in the hall a few feet away. It wasn't a very long phone call.

It didn't have to be.

Yes, there was the sex. If I'm honest there was never very much else.

*

It was about halfway through the news that the item about David Irving came on. I think he'd just lost a libel case. Something like that. I wasn't paying a great deal of attention. There were some shots of him hurrying away from the court and some archive footage, including Irving giving the Nazi salute at, what looked like, a National Front rally.

I shifted a little on the sofa and Sarah sat up and put her arm around my neck. "Bastard," I said.

"What?"

"David Irving. I really hate him. The worst thing is how he hides behind all that pseudo-intellectual bullshit. At least most of the other mouth breathers in the NF and BNP have got an excuse. They're as thick as shit."

By my standards it was quite a rant.

Sarah pulled her arm from my shoulder. "I see," she said. Her mouth was set in a thin line.

"What's up?" I said.

She wouldn't look at me. "Nothing. Just a difference of opinion. I'm sure it doesn't matter."

I paused a moment, letting the implication sink in. "You're not telling me you sympathise with him, are you?" I pointed at the screen, although the Irving story had finished and now the screen was full of an earthquake in Mexico.

"There's no need to raise your voice. I just think he asks some interesting questions. It's the done thing not to listen."

"That's bollocks, Sarah. He's been shot down in flames time and time again. He's just a sad old Hitler groupie."

"I thought you had an open mind."

"I have. So they didn't gas anyone at Auchswitz, then? Hitler had no idea about the Death Camps?"

She shrugged. "I don't know for sure. Neither do you."

"How about the National Front and Combat 18. Have they got a point, as well? I never took you for a racist, Sarah."

"I don't see myself that way," she said quietly. She paused, then she said, "I've been to BNP rally's. I used to be a member."

I sat and stared at her with my mouth open. She couldn't meet my eyes.

"I'm not ashamed of it," she said. "I'm not changing what I believe because of you."

"Nor should you," I said.

And that was pretty much that.

*

She left the next morning. We tried to talk, tried to make some sense of our differences, but suddenly there was no middle ground. We'd gone from intimacy to utter alienation in the blink of an eye. I asked her if there was any chance that this was another passing phase, like soft drugs or casual sex, but she merely shook her head, avoided my eyes without smiling, without acknowledging at all the tiny bridge I was attempting to build across the chasm between us.

Withdrawal took about a month. The physical craving eased a little after that. Work helped. I was once more a model employee. I sold the flat and moved to the other side of the city. No matter how often I washed my bedclothes they still reeked of Sarah, so I threw them away and bought some more. I disposed of her favourite mug as well and some cutlery and plates.

It was a several more weeks before I noticed the missing cheques. I subsequently discovered that my bank accounts were a few hundred pounds light. Some other stuff was missing; a watch Helen gave me, a gold chain, a handful of CD's.

My mother never saw the grandchildren she craved. She died of a heart attack a year after Sarah left. I saw little of my mother in that time; her house, particularly the sofa, held too many memories.

*

A few days ago I saw Sarah's face for the first time in

three years. It was on page five of The Eastern Daily Press. It was a passport photo and it looked several years old. She looked young, but not innocent and her eyes were half open and cast downward. Her hair was longer than I remembered it and she'd tied it back in a ponytail. Her name, according to the story below the picture, was Rachael Kennedy and she'd been found dead in a patch of wasteland near Wicken Fen. Apparently her body was naked and she'd been strangled and sexually assaulted.

Little was known about Rachael Kennedy. She was twenty-five years old and she was a native of Felixstowe. She travelled around Australia in her late teens and it wasn't clear when she had returned to this country. It was thought she might have been using a different name. Her parents had proved impossible to trace. The police, who were appealing for witnesses, believed she was last seen hitching a lift at the side of the A14, between Cambridge and Bury St.Edmonds.

Later I showed the newspaper to Angela and told her everything about Sarah. Angela and I had been together for a year. We weren't yet living together, although we'd discussed it. I hadn't mentioned Sarah before and I was worried how Angela would react.

It was Saturday afternoon and we were in my flat. I was half watching cricket on TV with the sound turned down. England against the West Indies on Channel Four. Can't get used to commercial breaks every couple of overs. Gough had an lbw shout against Campbell turned down. It looked pretty close to me.

Finally Angela folded the paper in half and laid it on the coffee table. She asked me a couple of questions about Sarah, about our time together and I answered them. Then she said, "How do you feel about this?" She nodded at the paper. "Now she's dead."

I looked at her. She has short black hair and grey eyes and a kind smile. She's a farmer's daughter and her complexion is pink and healthy. She doesn't bother with make-up much. She doesn't need to.

I thought about lying. Then I said, "To be honest it's a relief. I know how that sounds, but it's the truth. I can stop wondering where she is, who she's with. But I'm sorry as well. She didn't deserve this." I looked at Angela then back at the TV. Gough had Campbell this time, taken at slip by Thorpe. "I tried to warn her about hitching. She just laughed. Said she'd been doing it as long as she could remember. Said she was a good judge of character."

"Perhaps she was. Most of the time."

"Perhaps."

"Are you going to call the police?"

"No. I should, but I'm not going to. I thought about it before, when I realised she'd stolen from me. But it didn't seem worth it then and it doesn't now."

I glanced at the TV again. After more adverts I realised it was the tea break. West Indies were thirty-six for two. I turned the television off.

Angela smiled and took my hand. "You know she was lying, don't you?"

"What? Her name? Yes, I..."

"No, all that Nazi stuff. She made it up."

"Why?"

"To make it easy for you, of course. I think she cared about you, Tim. More than she intended to, at least."

"What's this? Female intuition?"

"If you like. Think about it, Tim. She was a con artist. She was with you for three months, she had the run of your flat and all she took was a couple of hundred quid and a few trinkets. And that right wing stuff was a bit out of the blue, wasn't it? The way you tell it you had no idea. People like that aren't usually that subtle. She was a clever girl. She knew what buttons to press."

"What was the point? She could have up and left anytime she liked."

"So why didn't she? She cared for you, Tim. She was making it easy for you."

"Easy?"

"Well, it was easier than coming home from work to find her gone and your flat stripped bare."

"I suppose."

We were quiet for a moment. I looked into her grey eyes. "Does it bother you," I said. "All this."

She tilted her head to one side and smiled her warm smile. "Why should it? It's all history now, isn't it? The poor girl's dead now and that's that." She leaned over and kissed my cheek. "I'm glad you told me, though."

I hugged her and told her that I was glad too. Then I turned the TV on. Play had started again and Caddick had just had Lara caught behind.

Blind Spot

"We can't do this," Flick said, shrugging off her bra and dropping it by the side of the bed.

"I know," I said. I sat inches from her, dressed in only my jeans, guilt radiating away from me.

I couldn't take my eyes off her. I'd seen her breasts before of course, on the beach in Spain, a couple of summers back. I'd spent a week with her and Frank, shared a villa with them, heard them making love through my thin bedroom wall.

But this was different. She sat with her shoulders hunched forward and her face tilted towards me. Her mouth was half-open and her eyes, huge and round and darker than ever, were full of light.

"We just can't," she said, adjusting her balance slightly, laying her hand on my shoulder for support and peeling off her white cotton knickers in a single movement. She dropped them next to her bra. She stared at me defiantly, her hands in her lap. There was a primness about her despite her nakedness and something about her perfectly proportioned slenderness and the way the muted light from the bedside lamp caught her hair and made her pale skin glow as though lit from within that almost stopped my breath.

"Jesus Christ," I said, reaching for her, stroking her neck, her hair. Kissing her mouth, tasting the wine she'd had earlier, finding her teeth and her tongue.

She pulled away slightly and tugged at my jeans. "Let's get these off."

I put a hand on her arm. "Actually, we really can't."

She smiled at me. "Right," she said, "as if we can stop."

"He'll know," I said.

"He's four hundred miles away. He won't know unless we tell him. And, believe me, I'm not going to tell him."

"He'll know," I said again.

She put her arms around me, linking her fingers behind my neck. She kissed the top of my head. She waited until I looked up, into her eyes. They were wide and bright and deeper than they had any right to be. "We're owed this, Chris. Have been for years. Let's just enjoy it."

My hands were on her waist. I kept them still. My erection thrust painfully against my jeans. "Is this just a one off, then? I couldn't handle that, Flick."

"You think I could?"

"I don't know what to think."

She put her hand between my legs. I winced. "Just think with this for once in your life." She kissed the stubble on my chin, then buried her face in my neck. I felt her hand in my lap and the warmth of her breath on my throat. I smelt the perfume she always wore. I looked past her shoulder at the open door and the shadows in the landing beyond.

*

A week earlier I'd let Frank beat me at squash. It was the usual story. We were at the Oasis club out on the Thorpe Road. I gave him the run around in the first two games. Pinging the ball into the corners, controlling the T, hearing his heavy laboured lunges behind me. His face was purple, his smile a grimace and his breath came in ragged rasps. Then, as usual, I eased off. Let him claw his way back, point by point. It was hard, though. Every now and then I'd snap a forehand past him and watch him flounder in the corner. Then I'd turn my back to him, in case he saw the expression on my face.

At last I sliced an easy backhand into the tin at match point in the fifth.

"Good game, Chris. You nearly had me that time." Frank slapped his hand on my shoulder, digging his thick fingers in.

"Yeah, nearly. Next time, perhaps."

"Dream on, mate. I never lose. I thought you knew that."

He grinned at me. His face was still brick red, his airtex shirt dark with sweat. "Good work-out though. Just what I needed." He grinned at me again. His face was round and plump and could have been pleasant if it wasn't for the greed that shone in his eyes.

His arm was still around me and he pulled me close. He stank of sweat and of something else I couldn't place. I almost admired the old bastard's arrogance. He was pushing fifty, short, at least three stone overweight. He was powerful, though. He'd boxed in his youth and the strength was evident still in his vast arms and across his shoulders and in his neck, which was as thick as my upper thigh.

But I had fifteen years on him and I was as fit as I'd ever been. I'd played squash to County standard in my twenties and have coached on and off since. But still he convinced himself that he beat me on merit week after week.

Not that I had the guts to contradict him, of course.

We showered and changed and Frank had me drive his Merc to the café at the city end of Hall Road. "We'll have breakfast there," he said. "With proper people. Can't stand those ponces at the club."

I could've pointed out that he didn't have to be a member, but instead I just nodded, like a good boy.

We took a table near the window, where I could keep an eye on the car. The café smelled of cooking fat and coffee and cigarette smoke drifted across to us from the counter. I could see the newsagent's and the fishmonger's across the road. Outside it was early autumn and the air was clear and cold and smelled of apples.

Tony, the owner, recognised Frank, as did a few of the regulars. They smiled their greetings with all the sincerity of a whore's kiss, but Frank lapped it up. He waved back at them as though bestowing a Papal blessing.

He had a full fried breakfast with half a dozen slices of white bread and a mug of tea with three sugars. On the house, of course. I had granary toast and orange juice.

He saw me looking at his breakfast. "What?"

"Why do even bother visiting your doctor?"

"What the fuck does he know. He's probably got a drug habit. When I was starting out quacks were among my best customers. When you could get the tight bastards to pay."

He saw me looking at him. "You're changing the subject."

"I've had my exercise, haven't I? A man's got to eat. Christ, you're a worse nag than Flick. Life's too short, I tell you."

"Be a whole lot shorter, you keep eating shit like that."

"Bollocks," he said, his mouth full of sausage and bacon. He ate quickly and noisily. It was like watching a pig at a trough. He had his head bent over the plate, presumably so he could get the food to his mouth that much more quickly. I could see where his dark hair was thinning on top. He had it trimmed short at the sides. He wore a mauve shell-suit with a navy T-shirt. His thick chest hair welled above the neck. There was a heavy gold chain around his throat and a couple of chunky gold rings on his equally chunky fingers. He stank of testosterone.

When he'd finished he sat back, pushed the plate to one side, wiped his mouth with the back of his hand.

"Here, Tony. Chuck us a Kit-Kat, mate."

Tony brought the chocolate over and poured more tea into Frank's mug. Frank ate the Kit-Kat in three bites and washed it down with tea. Then he lit a cigarette, sighed and looked across at me. "What's up, Chris? You've a hardly touched your toast. Got to eat, a growing boy like you."

I shrugged. "I'll grab something later. No big deal."

"Got to feed the inner man. You're probably going down with something. You look like shit."

"Cheers."

"I need you fit. No good to me sick. What's up with you?"

"Nothing," I said, tearing my toast into small pieces and staring at my hands.

"Whatever," he said. "Anyway, I've got a trip coming up."

I looked at him. "Where?"

"Glasgow."

"Glasgow?"

He looked at me. "It's a city. In Scotland."

"Yeah, yeah. What's in Glasgow?"

"Porn. Complete filth. Those Gorbals girls will do anything for a deep-fried Mars Bar. And I mean anything."

"Why are we going? You could send Brian and Terry to pick up a few tapes."

"The guy who's selling is an old mate of mine. We've got some catching up to do. And I said I. Not we. I need you here."

"Why?"

"You need a rest. You've been working too hard."

"But the VAT man's coming to the club on Friday."

"Gayle can do it. The paperwork's done, isn't it?" I nodded. "Just make sure she's got the right set of books and wears a short skirt and there won't be a problem. Keep away from the club for a while." He finished his tea and drummed his thick fingers on the tabletop. "Actually, you can do me a favour. Keep an eye on Flick for me."

"Flick?"

"Yeah. She's been a bit strange recently. Dunno why." He grinned at me. There was stubble on his chin and his teeth were white. "She might open up to you. You can take her shopping and stuff. She's always had a soft spot for you. I think you're the big brother she never had."

"I'll do my best," I said, avoiding his eyes.

"Good. I'm leaving Friday and I'll be gone at least a week. There's some other stuff up there I want to look into.

I'll fill you in when I get back. I'll take Brian along. Terry can help Gayle at the club."

"Fine."

A little later we walked to the car. The air was cold and sweet.

"Tell you what," Frank said, tossing me the car keys. "We'll go somewhere nice for lunch. Adlard's or Prince's Inn. Get some decent grub. That fry-up was fucking shit. You ought to raise your sights a bit, mate." He pointed a finger at me, grinning across the Mercedes roof.

It was just after five when I got home and Gayle was sitting on the sofa, legs tucked beneath her, reading a magazine. She jumped up when she saw me. She looked scared and guilty. "God, Chris, you're early. I haven't cooked yet." She looked at her watch. Her eyes were wide open. "Shit, you're not early, are you? I lost track of time, Chris. I'm sorry." She wrung her hands together. "I'm sorry," she said again.

I moved towards her and she flinched away from me. I put my hand gently on her shoulder. "It's all right, love. It's not a problem. I'll get us a takeaway or something." I pulled her to me and she buried her head in my shoulder. Her hair smelt odd. She didn't wash it quite as often as she should. "How long have we been together?" I said. "Almost a year now. Have I ever hurt you?"

I felt her head move as she sobbed into my armpit. Gayle was Frank's niece. She was twenty-three. When she was seventeen, on the verge of her A Levels, she hitched to London one night and her family didn't see her again for almost two years. She was picked up by a small-time pimp and heroin addict called Carver. By the time Frank traced them to a squat on the Manor estate in Sheffield Gayle was so wasted on speed and low-grade heroin that she didn't recognise him. I bundled her into the back of Frank's car. She screamed and clawed at me. She stank of vomit and old sweat. When I found Frank he had Carver pinned against an alley wall and was punching him repeatedly in the stomach. When he pulled away I saw the blood and the glint of steel. Frank stared straight through me. Brian and I cleaned him up and got him out of there.

Frank never mentioned Sheffield after that. I don't know how he did it or what strings he pulled, but nothing that happened that night ever worked its way back to him.

And I ended up with Gayle. Or she ended up with me. Frank thought it was a good idea and that was that. She was bright

and pretty and pulled her weight behind the bar and in the
office at Frank's club, but emotionally she was a blank canvas.
She was burnt out, empty and fragile. Her opinions were likely
to be that of the last person she'd spoken to.

"Are you sure you're not angry?" she said, looking up
at me. Her face was white, her brown eyes soft and tired.

"Don't be silly," I said, easing her away from me. "Dig
out that menu from the Chinese, will you love? I'll phone
something through."

She beamed at me and went into the kitchen. I felt a
small stab of guilty relief when she was out of my sight.

I worked my way slowly through the plate of sweet and
sour chicken and fried rice. Gayle picked at hers occasionally.
She looked better once she'd showered and washed her hair. It
shone now; it was long and dark and fell to her shoulders. She
smelt faintly of lemons.

I told her I'd be away from the club for a while and she
nodded. "You can handle the VAT man, can't you? On Friday."

"Can I?"

"Of course you can. I get the impression that Frank's
shaved the dice."

"What?"

I sighed. "He's paid someone off. Just look pretty and
make sure he gets the right papers. It's a formality."

"What have you got to do?" she said.

"Frank wants me to look after Flick."

"Oh."

"Is that a problem?"

"No, no," she said without looking at me.

After a pause I said, "I don't like it anymore than you do."

She gave me a look that said, "we both know that's
bollocks," but kept her mouth shut.

A little later I said, "You know, Gayle, between you and
me, I think Frank's losing it"

"You say that every night," she said, smiling a little.

I nodded and smiled back. She was right. I did.

The evening before Frank left for Glasgow I drove Flick
home from the club. It was raining when we hit the narrow road
between Mattishall and Frank's house in Yaxham. It was almost
midnight and I was tired and it was hard to see through the
blurred Norfolk darkness. It was drowsily warm in the Mercedes.
According to the dashboard it was only four degrees outside.

The car was full of Flick's scent. It still would be days later. She'd said little during the drive, just sat with her legs crossed, humming along to whatever song played on the radio.

She wore a honey-coloured three-quarter length fake fur coat over a crimson evening dress. She wore dark stockings and black high-heeled shoes. Her lip-gloss matched the colour of her dress; the make-up around her eyes made them sparkle darkly. Her blonde hair was quite short, cut in a loose bob. I tried not to look at her. I didn't always succeed.

I pulled the Mercedes into her drive and cut the engine. Without the radio and the hushed roar of the heater the silence was startling. Flick didn't move.

"Looking forward to next week?" she said, and I jumped at the sound of her voice. "When the cat's away and all that."

I shrugged. "Makes no difference to me. What about you?"

"I can't pretend I'll miss him." She paused a moment. "Actually, that's not true. I'll have to pretend I miss him. That's my job, after all."

"Poor little rich girl."

She laughed, was quiet for a moment, then said, "I thought you were my friend. You don't talk to me anymore."

"What's to say, Flick? What the fuck do want me to say?"

I stared through the windscreen at the sweep of the drive and the outline of the house, hidden in shadow.

"I've seen the way you look at me."

"I look at lots of women. I'm weak that way."

"You can't look at me now, can you? If you didn't feel anything for me this wouldn't be so difficult."

"It's you who's making it difficult."

She'd kept her voice light, detached until then, but now her hand gripped my arm. She wore no gloves and her nails were painted the colour of wine. When she spoke her voice was animated and I could feel her eyes on my face. "I know what you want, Chris. I want it, too. It's up to us. We're adults, after all. We can do as we please."

"That's a good joke, Flick."

She squeezed my arm. "Remember when you kissed me last Christmas? Frank was in the next room. I thought you were so brave."

"I was pissed."

"So was I. Do you think that mattered? I remember how you kissed me, the look in your eyes. I'm not stupid, Chris."

"I know. But what if you say is true? It changes nothing."

She withdrew her hand and sat in silence for a moment. "Perhaps I've misjudged you," she said at last.

"What does that mean?"

Another pause, then, "He's not God, you know."

"He may as well be. Look, most of the time I detest the old bastard, but I owe him. And," I closed my eyes, "I'm scared of him. Let's face it, we all are."

"Anyone with half a brain would be. But the thing is, you've got less to worry about than any of us."

"How do you work that out?"

"You must have noticed Frank's blind spots, Chris. Like his health. He thinks he's immortal. He's got a dodgy ticker, right? So what does he do? He plays squash once a week, does half an hour on the exercise bike, perhaps manages the occasional shag if I'm really out of luck. He still smokes. Still drinks. Eats any shit he fancies, but that's OK, he's Frank Plummer. He can't have a heart attack. He's made up his mind. He's like that about you, Chris. You're one of his blind spots."

"Me?"

"He thinks the sun shines out of your arse. Makes me sick sometimes. Chris this and Chris that. He thinks of you as a son." I grimaced. "He's grooming you to be his successor."

"Jesus Christ."

"You're as safe as houses, Chris. He'd never blame you for anything. It'll always be someone else's fault. Blaming you would be like blaming himself. And Frank never does that."

"He still frightens me."

"You're a spineless bastard, Chris."

"I know."

"But I still want you. What does that make me?"

I said nothing.

"I want you to have dinner with me. Next Wednesday. Seven-thirty. I'll cook us something nice."

I stared at my hands on the steering wheel. I wanted her to go. I wanted her to lean across and put her tongue in my mouth. I didn't know what the hell I wanted.

"Will you come?" she said.

Perhaps it was the sadness in her voice. I closed my eyes and took a deep breath. "How can I refuse," I said.

The next morning I dropped Frank and Brian at the airport. Frank was in a foul mood. He kept finding reasons to bollock us both, even though we'd long taken the hint and kept our mouths shut. Brian took it all without flinching. He'd heard it all before. He was Frank's age, built like a mountain, with eyes like flint and a thin mouth that never smiled.

Although I was used to Frank's moods it bothered me. I wondered what Flick had said to him. I tried to push her from my thoughts and failed. She disturbed me. Thinking of her left me vulnerable and unbalanced.

I watched the plane take off, gain height above the outskirts of Norwich. Although I'd seen families with small children among the passengers boarding with Frank and Brian I still found myself hoping that it would crash.

*

Flick's fingers fumbled with my jeans, her mouth warm against my chest. I stroked her hair and her back. Her skin was hot. I closed my eyes and opened them again.

Frank stood in the doorway. Brian was with him, and another man, someone I didn't know. I hadn't heard a car or their footsteps on the stairs. They still made no noise. Frank looked straight at me and there was no expression on his face.

I froze and it was this that made Flick look up. She seemed to wither in front of me. She said, "Oh God," three times quickly and put her hand to her mouth.

I inched away from her. I could still taste her and smell her hair, but I inched myself backwards, tried to distance myself from her. As if it would make any difference.

"I'm sorry," Flick said. I'm not sure who she was speaking to. Her voice trembled and her face was white.

Frank looked right through her. He moved across to me and put his hand on my shoulder. "Up you get," he said. "Put some clothes on." His voice was as empty as his expression. "This is Carl, by the way," he said, nodding at the stranger. Carl was tall and broad, with a pale face and black hair slicked back and tied in a ponytail.

I pulled a sweater on and adjusted my trousers. My erection was a distant memory. My legs felt like water when I stood.

"Carl, you stay with Flick. Chris, you come with me and Brian," Frank said. His voice was flat, his eyes hooded.

I followed them through the door. I glanced back once. The last I saw of Flick she sat motionless, her head bowed. Carl stood a couple of feet away, his hands by his sides.

Brian pulled the bedroom door shut. He didn't look at me. "Downstairs," Frank said. I walked between them. I wanted to plead, to make excuses, but I could think of nothing to say.

Frank told me to wait in the kitchen. The sink and draining board were littered with the debris of the meal that Flick had cooked. Our wineglasses were next to the kettle.

I thought of running, but I didn't think my legs would carry me. And I realised that I no longer cared what happened.

Frank came in and threw me my coat. "Come on, Chris. We're going to the club. Get ourselves a drink."

"What?"

"You heard me."

"Right. Going for a drive in the country, are we? Find some woods? Somewhere nice and isolated."

He smiled and shook his head and spread his hands out in front of him. "You've got it all wrong, mate. We'll just have a drink. Put this behind us."

"And what is this, exactly? Some kind of test?"

"Yes. A test. And you passed."

"I passed?"

He looked at me. "It was Flick that failed."

"I don't get it. I was just about to fuck your wife. You can't put it all on her."

He turned his head away and grimaced. He leant back against the Aga, folding his arms in front of him. "There's a camera in the light fitting, Chris. We watched it all on the PC in the study."

I felt my face burn and I couldn't meet his eyes.

"You were a soldier in there, Chris. You really were. If the situation was reversed and it was your wife coming on to me? And she looked as good as Flick? I'd have fucked her in an instant. No offence."

"I'm living with your niece."

"But you take my point. For a moment in there I wondered if you were gay." He smiled and his smile had all the colour and flavour of ice.

"What happens to Flick?"

This time he couldn't meet my eyes. "The thing about women is, they have all the power. Us men, we're led by our dicks. You show me a man who says he's not led by his dick and I'll show you a liar." He looked at the floor. "She dealt the cards. You didn't stand a chance."

"That's bollocks. What happens to her, Frank?"

He shrugged. "You decide. Believe what you want to believe. Whatever gets you through. What happens, happens. Some things we can't control."

"And that's that?"

He leant towards me and I flinched away from his stale breath. "I need you, Chris. You're my right hand man. I've got big plans for you." He pulled away again. "I'm going for a drink. You can come now or you can wait here. Carl will be down shortly."

He looked at me briefly without expression, then walked out of the door. I followed.

When I got home it was almost three in the morning and Gayle was waiting up for me, as she always did when I was late home. She sat on the sofa in her pink towelling robe and Winnie the Pooh slippers. The usual fear was in her eyes and she said nothing.

"You don't have to wait up for me, Gayle. I'm a big boy now."

"What's the matter?"

"Nothing's the matter. Why does something always have to be the matter? For fucks sake."

Her eyes widened and she was close to tears. I hated myself but I couldn't stop. I grabbed her arm and pulled towards the doorway.

"Come on. You're coming upstairs with me."

"Why?"

"Why do you think?"

She stopped for a moment and looked at me. She tried to smile. "This is a game, isn't it, Chris?"

She climbed the stairs. "Yeah," I said, "that's right, Flick. It's a game."

"You called me, Flick."

"No, I didn't. Gayle. I said Gayle."

She glanced back at me. She was about to argue, but she saw the expression on my face and changed her mind.

In the bedroom she took off her dressing gown. I pushed her onto the bed. She was wet when I entered her. I'd wanted her to be dry. I'd wanted to force my way in.

I thrust at her without love or consideration and all the time she smiled up at me. I turned my face away. I thought of Flick as I came.

*

The squash court stinks of Frank's sweat. He has his hands on his knees and he's looking up at me. His face is grey, his eyes dark and sunken.

"Fucking hell, Chris. What are you trying to do? Kill me?"

I look back at him and my smile feels like an open wound. "Yeah, that's right. I'm really going to kill my meal ticket, aren't I? This is just what the doctor ordered. A fucking good workout."

He straightens with some difficulty and tosses me the ball. "Your serve."

"You know, Frank, I think I might win this one."

"Like fuck you will," he says, but I've already served, a slow lob that drops past his backhand. I hear the squeak of his shoes as he turns on the wooden floor and the laboured rasp of his breathing as he chases the ball into the far corner.

For The Love Of A Taciturn Man

The air is steel cold as I fetch the pint of semi-skimmed from the doorstep of my terraced house. My small front lawn is white and rutted and reminds me of the corrugated iron roofs on the outbuildings of my father's old farm. It's the first week of the new year and winter has only just started to bite. Not that I'm sorry. I turned seventy a fortnight ago and I feel the cold. I shiver a little, pull my cardigan tighter around me and turn up the heating.

I suppose I'm lucky as far as pensioners go. The house is paid for, I've a small occupational pension and a little money in the bank. I keep warm. I eat well. I take a bath or a shower every day. Consequently I don't smell of piss like so many old people I know, particularly the woman who invariably joins me in the pension queue at the Post Office every Thursday.

Also, unlike this woman, I don't constantly decry the younger generation or drone on and on about how much better things were in my day. I usually smile and nod as she speaks.

It's easier that way.

I live alone, which I enjoy. As I approach the end of my life I'm probably happier than I have ever been. Although all things are relative, of course.

*

My brother and I never knew the name of the man we watched our father murder in the spring of 1944. He was a travelling salesman of some sort; brushes, pots and pans, I'm not sure what. Either I don't remember or I never knew in the first place. He was small and neat. Back then we thought he was old, but I suppose he was barely in his forties. The same age as our father, a little older than our mother. He had black hair, Brylcremed back, and a small moustache. I still remember his cruel smile, although later, when I mentioned it to Gordon, he had no recollection of it. He thought I was somehow trying to excuse Father's actions.

Perhaps I was. But then I knew things that Gordon didn't.

Home Farm, which had been in our family since the turn of the century, was set in a slice of Norfolk wilderness between a triangle of villages perhaps half a dozen miles from the

Suffolk border. It was a small farm. A few pigs, some chickens, a house cow. A couple of strawberry fields, patches of raspberry cane. We harvested wheat and barley in the autumn, sugar beet in the winter.

My father used casual labour when it was needed. Gordon and I spent school holidays and most weekends working on the fields or feeding animals and sometimes we'd have Italian prisoners of war working alongside us. My father lived to work. Dawn to dusk and on the Sabbath as well, which was rare and frowned upon in those days and in our part of the country. He didn't believe in God. I don't think this was due to deep reflection on his part, he simply didn't have time for what he considered a frippery. It was ironic. He was in many ways the archetypal Protestant; work obsessed, relentlessly dour, rigidly anti-pleasure.

He was a sullen, ill-tempered brute of a man, but I loved him anyway.

*

Back in the kitchen I make a mug of tea and drink it at the table. I eat wholemeal toast and browse through the sports pages of The Guardian. I am the last remaining member of my family. When I die the Walton name dies with me. I don't consider it a burden. I've never married, Gordon did but he couldn't have children. He died in 1977. He was driving alone on the small road between Swardeston and Mulbarton when his car hit a tree. It was late at night and his body wasn't discovered until the next morning.

He lives on in my dreams, as do my mother and my father. And the man my father killed.

*

Gordon and I were making a cart of sorts from pram wheels and old planks when we first saw him. It was a Saturday afternoon in March and it was cold and the sun was low in a hard blue sky. He was wearing a dark coat that was long in the sleeves. He held his hat in one hand and placed his battered briefcase on the floor of our porch while he knocked on the door. As he waited he smoothed his oiled hair back on his scalp. The door opened a little and our mother ushered him inside. We had no idea where our father was. It was good to have a couple of hours to ourselves at the weekend and we played on a worn, scruffy patch of land that separated the house from the first of our fields.

"Who was that?" Gordon said. He was trussing a bent wheel to a makeshift axle with some old rope. He looked up at me, his cheeks red in spite of the cold.

I shrugged. "Dunno. Is it the tallyman?"

"Don't think so," Gordon said. "Hold this for me, Brian. I can't get it tight enough." Gordon was two years younger than me. He was slimmer too, better looking in a pretty kind of way. He had floppy blond hair and a lopsided grin. I took after father. Tall and broad with jet-black hair. I tried to smile frequently to offset the sulleness of my features. Gordon said it made me look simple.

Whoever the man was we soon forgot him. Absorbed in our ramshackle construction we barely noticed when father appeared about twenty minutes later. He was coatless, with his sleeves rolled up. His braces held his trousers ludicrously high on his stomach. He glowered at us.

"Is that man still here?" he said.

"Who is he, Dad?" Gordon said. I glanced at him, giving the smallest shake of my head.

Dad paused and looked at Gordon. He didn't raise his voice but the tone changed a fraction. "I said, is that man still here."

"Yes Dad, he is." I said quickly.

He nodded. "You two come with me. There's work to do." He turned his back and walked away from us. We dropped the pieces of our cart and followed him.

I saw the stranger again about a fortnight later. I was walking home along the village road, head down, hands in pockets, thinking about nothing in particular. I was about half a mile from our house when he passed me. He wore a suit that was baggy in the arms and legs and a black hat. His face was red. He smiled and winked at me as he passed. I turned and watched him go.

*

Later in the morning I sit at the table in the living room with a cup of instant coffee and two dark chocolate digestive biscuits and watch a Robin and a pair of Blue Tits squabble over bacon rind on the bird table in the garden. Radio Four plays in the background, but I scarcely hear it. I think of Gordon. His smile and his blue eyes and his blond hair that our mother loved to touch. In fact she could hardly pass Gordon without touching him; a hand on his shoulder, a kiss on the cheek. My mother barely touched me at all as far as I can remember. I probably reminded her too much of my father.

Gordon and I had picnics of jam sandwiches and cold tea and the tiny, intensely sweet pears we plucked from the tree in our small orchard. Once, as we were eating, a Messerschmitt 109 roared over us, hedgehopping towards the coast. We flinched at the sheer bowel trembling power of it. Within seconds it was a speck and we sat opened mouthed, recalling the swastika decals, the sky blue painted underside, the mottled drab olive fuselage. It was about as close as the war got to us, although the American air base at Honingham was strafed and bombed a few weeks later.

There is still ice on the water I put out for the birds the night before. My garden is long and thin and mist lingers among the branches of the apple tree towards the garden's end. I think I see a child in the mist. A slender boy with blond hair, wearing a collarless shirt and a striped sleeveless sweater and knee-length shorts. His head tilts to one side slightly, at the same angle as his grin.

I remember Gordon's smile so well and the look of sheer, wide-eyed terror on his face as our father...

*

...yanked the small man through the threshold of our front door by the collar of his dark suit and dragged him past us towards the outbuildings at the bottom of the path. We'd been playing football. Our mother's face was framed by a square of curtain at the kitchen window. Gordon and I looked at each other and I'm sure that the slack-jawed horror on his face was mirrored on my own. It was a mid-April day, cool and dull, but our father's rage seemed to burn through the low cloud and bathe us all in a sulphurous light. He paused and turned towards us. He held the small man by the scruff of the neck, as one would carry a rabbit or a cat. The muscles in my father's arms and neck and shoulders stood out as though sculpted. The man's face was a deep red, his eyes wide open. His tie was askew, the collar of his shirt pulled tight against his throat. Our father turned away from us again and continued dragging the small, terrified man, his feet kicking and scrabbling for purchase on the dusty path, towards the outbuildings.

God help us, we followed.

There was a full water butt set against the junction of the barn and the old stable. Gordon and I used to peer into its cold depths and marvel at the strange tiny creatures that swam there. By the time our father reached it he was breathing heavily and he hurled the stranger against the stable wall. He bounced off and fell to his knees, clawing at the tie at his throat and whimpering.

And we thought that was that. Perhaps Dad would punch him a couple of times and perhaps we wanted him to. Then it would be over.

But Father gathered himself, glowered at the broken mess in front of him and then at us, his brow as low and dark as a thunderhead. He hesitated for a moment, as though he was trying to summon words he couldn't find. Then he took the cowering man by the throat, lifted him to shoulder height and dunked him head first into the water butt.

Green water cascaded over the side. All we could see of the man were his legs from the knee down and they thrashed frantically, sometimes catching our father in the face or head, but he didn't flinch. He just held him there, his arm thrust into the water up to the shoulder and eventually the kicking weakened and then stopped. He held him there another minute, turned his face to us and said, "Fetch the barrow."

As usual we did as we were told. He dumped the body face up in the barrow. Water gushed from the nose and mouth.

Gordon was crying now. I put my arm around him and he sobbed on my shoulder.

Just before he wheeled the barrow down the small slope towards the copse of pear and apple trees our father turned to us and said, "You speak to no-one of this. Ever."

It was a statement, not a request. And it was probably the most unnecessary statement I've ever heard.

*

After lunch I submit to my addiction. I watch "Neighbours" and "Home and Away". I like the sunshine and the girls are pretty.

Our mother died in the summer of 1945. Gordon and I came home from the fields one weekend afternoon to find her curled in a foetal position on the kitchen floor. She'd choked to death on a piece of apple.

Quite abruptly, just after the war, Dad sold the farm and we moved into a terraced house in Great Yarmouth. He got a job as a tea salesman. He trundled around the Norfolk countryside, visiting Greengrocers and General Stores in his red Trojan van with the Brooke Bond livery on the side. Our house stank of the tea he kept stored in our back room. Despite being an unlikely salesman he did quite well. Wordless intimidation obviously worked for him.

By the early Fifties Gordon and I had both completed our National Service. Gordon joined the RAF and was posted abroad.

I got a job as a clerk at the Borough Council.

I still lived with my father and sometimes, during my holidays, I would accompany him on his rounds. The van stank of tea and engine oil and the seats were hard and the suspension minimal. And my father still seethed with a silent, hidden rage. Despite this I relished the days we spent together. He no longer scared me. He'd grown fat since he'd given up physical work, although he was still massively powerful. And I felt that whoever the anger he nurtured inside himself was directed at, it wasn't at me.

*

One October Friday afternoon when the clouds were low and a cold wind rattled around the cab of dad's old Trojan he pulled into one of the passing spots on the coast road a couple of miles from Sheringham. I pulled my coat tighter around me and looked across at him. He stared out at the bare heath to his left. His eyes were still black and fierce but they seemed smaller now, set back in folds of fat. His jowls were red and his shirt collar chafed against his neck. We'd barely exchanged a word all day. Silences were normal. But now I knew that he wanted to speak and I knew, with equal certainty, that I did not want to listen.

"That man," he said, "the one I drowned. Do you remember?"

I looked away from him, taken aback by the subject and by the stupidity of the question. "I'm hardly likely to forget him, am I?"

"You'd be surprised," he said. "You can forget anything if you try hard enough."

I didn't reply. I hoped that if I just stared at a particular patch of purple heather for long enough and said nothing perhaps he'd give up and we could go back to our safe, familiar silence.

"I had my reasons," he said.

"I don't want to know."

"Well, you're going to," he said, quite gently. He was quiet again and I was just starting to think that perhaps he'd thought better of the whole idea when he said, "You're my son, Brian."

He said it as though it was a revelation and I turned to look at him again. He wouldn't meet my eyes.

"My only son."

I frowned.

"Gordon's not mine, boy. I thought you'd have guessed that years ago."

Well, I hadn't. I sat with my mouth open.

"After we had you I couldn't...well, it soon became obvious I wouldn't be a father again." He put a huge hand to his face and rubbed his eyes slowly. "Frankly boy, you weren't enough. I needed more sons. To help on the farm."

"That's enough," I said. But my voice was weak, pathetic and he ignored me.

"Your mother was an attractive woman. I arranged for one of the labourer's to call on her. It was all my idea. She wasn't keen. I made her. I thought I could cope with it. And I suppose I did. For a while."

"You treated her like a brood mare."

"Yes. Yes, I did. God forgive me."

"But you don't believe in God," I said.

"I do now," he said and stared across at me and for a moment I thought he was going to touch me, but he didn't.

"But after that one time she said she couldn't do it again. Flat refused. I was relieved. It tore me apart thinking of her with that bloody labourer. Then, in the middle of the war, she announces she wants a daughter. Just like that. So I asked her what she thought I could do about it and she says I can do what I did before. Find her a man."

"Stop. Please stop," I said.

"I can't stop," he said. "You're the only one I can tell." He closed his eyes and carried on. "She went on and on, she did. Wouldn't leave it alone. So in the end I found her someone. A right weasel, he was, I didn't think she'd have the stomach for it. But she did. More than once. And that's what I couldn't take. So I killed the bastard."

"And buried him in the orchard."

He nodded. "Don't know why I chose there. Bloody hard digging, what with all those roots and all. But I buried him deep enough. He's still there, as far as I know."

We sat in silence for a long time then drove on to Sheringham and sold some more tea.

I'd found a place of my own within a week. Dad started going to church every Sunday. I visited him every month or so and I was by his side when he died, riddled with cancer, in his mid-sixties. Even at the end his eyes still burned with the same sullen rage, a rage that I finally realised was turned inward, just as it had always been.

*

As dusk gathers I draw the curtains and turn the TV on again. There's a Harry Enfield Christmas Special on later that I'll probably watch. For supper I have boil in the bag cod with parsley sauce and mashed potatoes.

I feel tired and a little dizzy. I've been prescribed tablets for a heart condition. I should take two a day, but I keep forgetting.

Helen Said

The last thing Helen said to me? "Call me when you're sober."
That was two years ago and I haven't called her yet. In all
honesty I can't. To me sobriety is a concept, a theory,
something that happens to someone else. Not that I envy them.

*

Today I'm drinking mostly pints of Guinness with the
occasional whisky chaser.

I'm in the back room of the Yellow Rose on Newmarket
Street. It's a Saturday afternoon in May and outside it's
probably sunny and warm; it was earlier, it has been for days
now. It's cool in the bar, the red velvet curtains are drawn
and a fan turns listlessly on the whitewashed ceiling. The bar
is quiet, too; the jukebox and the fruit machine in the corner
are silent. Lenny and I sit on our usual bar stools and nurse
our drinks. Lenny's a friend. Technically. Pretty much my only
one.   We meet most days, chat a little, drink a lot. That's
close enough to a friend in my world.

"Amateurs," Lenny says, as a young couple slope off into
the sunlight after a quick half.

"No stamina," I say. "Imagine, choosing fresh air and
sunshine over this place."

"And our company," Lenny says.

"Young people today," I say. "No taste." I sip my
Guinness. I drink slowly. There's no rush, after all. Nothing
and no one to hurry for.

*

When I first met Helen she was working on reception in
a posh solicitor's office on Opie Street. I was a motorcycle
courier. I had a spate of deliveries to her office that summer,
six years ago. Papers, documents. I didn't know what they were,
didn't care, as long as Helen was there to sign for them. It
was four visits before I took my helmet off. As she said later,
it was downhill from then on.

*

Lenny belches softly. He's wearing a check shirt and a
pair of worn blue jeans. He's in his mid-fifties and looks ten
years older. I told him once he had a beer belly and he gave
me a look and said, he should fucking hope so, the gallons of

the stuff he'd put away. He spent most of his working life on the bins, for the council, until he took early retirement with a bad back two years ago. His arms are still thick with muscle, his shoulders broad. He puts his empty glass on the counter. It's four-thirty now and his eyes are soft and unfocused. "Get us another, mate," he says. There's white stubble on his cheeks and chin. He has that odd, slightly sour smell he always has these days.

I get him a pint of bitter. My Guinness is almost untouched so I buy myself a whisky to go with it. I sip it and close my eyes as it bites. Lenny drinks half of his pint in a single swallow. He looks at the counter. "That's better," he says.

*

"You look different without your leathers," Helen said, "and minus the helmet, of course."

It was our first date, in the wine bar off Bedford Street. I don't remember its name. I think it's closed now, anyway.

"Good different or bad different?" I said.

She tipped her head to one side and ran her finger along the rim of her wineglass. "Not sure yet. I'll let you know." She smiled. It was a good smile, all white teeth and dimpled cheeks.

I smiled back, aiming for wry and knowing, probably missing by a mile. "So kind," I said. "So very kind."

Helen was pretty, rather than beautiful, but her prettiness was concentrated, pared down, impossible to ignore. Her hair was blond and short, her eyes a vivid blue, her features symmetrical. She was small and slender and she dressed neatly, accentuating her compactness, her self-containment.

"Why Perrier?" she said, her finger resting on the bottle in front of me. "Doesn't quite fit with the butch biker image."

"Well, I'm not butch and I'm not a biker. Outside work, at least. Sorry to disappoint."

"So much for preconceptions. And who said I was disappointed? So, as I said, what's with the Perrier?"

"Nosy. I like the taste."

"What taste?"

I shrugged. "I'm driving."

She stared into her wineglass. "My father was an alcoholic." She paused and looked up at me.

I felt my cheeks redden. "I'm sorry."

"He wasn't," she said. "But I know the signs, that's all. Your complexion, your eyes, the broken veins. The slight shake in your right hand. The way you look at my wine."

I nodded and looked at the table. The bar was quiet and half-empty.

"I'm sorry," Helen said. "I can be a little forward."

"Just a little."

She smiled without embarrassment. "I'm not judging you or anything. I'm just a nosy sod. I like secrets, skeletons in cupboards."

"You like them?"

She nodded. "They hint at layers. At hidden depths."

"No depths here, love. I'm all shallows, me."

"We'll see," she said, still smiling. She rested her chin on her hand, tilting her face upwards. "Glad you asked me out?"

I sat back, drank some Perrier. "I'll tell you later."

"You were so nervous, weren't you? I wondered if you'd ever find the nerve."

"I couldn't believe you said yes. I was sure you'd have a boyfriend."

"Who says I haven't?"

"Good point."

She reached across and put her hand on my cheek. "Don't look that way. I'm just teasing, Mike. I do that a lot."

"Really? I'd never have guessed."

She laughed and drank some wine. Her lips were wet and there was a hint of colour in her cheeks.

*

Lenny calls it a day a little after eight. The fruit machine clatters occasionally. Dancing In The Moonlight plays on the jukebox.

As always before he leaves, Lenny buys Trish a drink. Trish is the barmaid. Our barmaid. She has short black hair, dark eyes and a kind heart. Trish is my other friend, I suppose. She's visited my flat a couple of times. We almost ended up in bed once; we didn't though, and I'm glad we didn't. It would have changed things. I need Trish as she is; mildly maternal, someone to lavish my self-pity on.

"Do you think you should see him home?" Trish says. She leans forward, her elbows on the bar. She wears a pink, scoop neck T-shirt and navy combat trousers. She's in her late twenties, a little younger than me.

"He'll be fine," I say. I can see him through the window, walking slowly and not entirely steadily. "He didn't hit it too hard."

"Right," Trish says. She gives me a look, dark eyes turned upward.

I drain my glass, consider going home myself. Saturday night TV. "I'll have another pint, Trish." My voice is steady enough, although things are pleasantly distant, blurred at the edges.

Trish wears a gold necklace with an amber pendant on it. She fingers the pendant, lifts it up, rubs it against her chin.

"Don't you think you've had enough?"

I sigh and waggle my glass in front of her. She sighs back and takes the glass, serves me my pint. She sips the coke that Lenny bought her and looks at her hands. It's a ritual we go through occasionally. She hectors me gently about my drinking from time to time. I need the illusion that she cares.

Once, at my flat, in the odd distorted hours just before dawn, as she nursed a cup of cold coffee, Trish asked me how much I drank.

I looked at her and shrugged. "What sort of question's that? I drink it all, Trish. As much as I can." I shrugged again and looked at my glass. "I drink with both hands, Trish. D'you know what I need? A funnel. That'd make life way easier." I blinked a couple of times and glanced up at her. She shook her head, sipped her coffee, didn't look back.

*

"Dad shot himself," Helen said. She sat in the elderly stuffed armchair in the living room of my flat, smoking a cigarette, gazing at the TV. We were watching Eastenders with the sound down. It's much better that way.

My head snapped up. "What?" We'd been talking about nothing much; music, work, what we planned that weekend.

"I was twelve. They came and fetched me from school." She frowned. "Double math's with Mr Murphy. He took his shotgun into the garage. Dad, that is, not Mr Murphy." She looked up, squinting through the smoke. "Put both barrels in his mouth. Pulled the trigger." She frowned again. "Mum was so angry. Still is."

"Jesus Christ. I don't know what to say."

She grinned too brightly, stubbed out her cigarette. "Nothing to say." She ran a hand through her hair, smoothed her black cotton skirt tight against her thighs. "It wasn't just the drink. He was terribly depressed." She glanced at me. "It was a long time before I found out what that really meant. And him and mum had been falling out for years. Apparently."

We'd been together six weeks. We hadn't slept together yet. I'd hoped that we would later that evening. Helen was different from the other girls I'd dated. Unreadable. She didn't sulk or get angry, but I felt constantly off balance, always at least one step behind.

"I'm sorry," she said. She looked into my eyes briefly, then back at the TV. "I don't know where that came from. I've made you feel awkward."

"No, no," I said quickly. A little too quickly, I expect. "You just caught me by surprise. You can talk to me about anything, you know that."

She shifted in her seat. She wore a powder-blue soft woollen sweater and I looked at her small breasts more often than I should. "You are a sweetheart." She paused, then said: "Why did you drink?"

"What?"

"I mean you've quit now, that's great, but I wondered why you drank in the first place." Her blue eyes were wide open and guileless. "And how did you quit? AA? On your own?"

I sat back in my chair, puffed my cheeks out, put a hand to my face. "Bloody hell, Helen."

"What's up? Question too hard?" There was no sarcasm in her voice. Her head tilted to one side and her eyes shone.

"Frankly, yes." I hesitated, stalling probably. "There isn't always a reason." My voice changed, thickened. Helen's face stayed the same. "There are no skeletons, Helen. No layers. No hidden depths." I sighed. I felt something dark and familiar and nameless circle within me. "I'm just a fuck-up, that's all. No excuses. All my own work."

She looked into my face and nodded. I looked away. After a moment she said, "Does it bother you that I drink? Can you taste it when you kiss me?"

I blinked a couple of times and smiled slowly. "Yes, I can taste it. And it bothers me sometimes. But never enough." She smiled back, leant forward, put a hand on my thigh. "Shall we go to bed?"

I nodded.

Later, she said, "You're not a fuck-up, Mike."
I said nothing and she held my hand in the darkness.

*

I say goodbye to Trish at nine-thirty. She gives me a nod and a half-smile. She knows she'll see me again tomorrow.

My flat is less than half a mile away. The air is thick

and warm and smells of flowers and fruit ripening. My head
buzzes slightly.

Later I sit in front of the TV; watch Total Recall and
take occasional sips from a bottle of Teachers. I've seen the
film before and found it only mildly diverting first time round.
Sharon Stone looks good though.

Later still I sleep fitfully and wake as I usually do;
thickheaded, bewildered, filled with a random, existential
dread.

I wash and shave and dress. I drink some water, take a
handful of Aspirin and a couple of nips from the Teacher's
bottle. Just to get the blood running.

I make some porridge and eat it slowly. I think of Helen
and look at the day through my kitchen window. The sun is bright
through the dirty glass and I squint against it.

*

Dry lightening flickered across the field to our left.
The sky was plum-coloured, the sky low and pregnant. It was a
Sunday afternoon in late October and Helen and I sat in her car
next to a wheatfield just outside Swardeston and waited for the
storm to break. We'd spent the day at the coast and were making
our way back to the city.

"I love storms," Helen said. Her face was still shiny
with grease from the chips we'd eaten on the seafront. I watched
her. Her eyes were on the clouds and the sudden, jagged
lightening. I had my window down and I could smell the
electricity in the air, taste it almost.

The wind was picking up, bullying the treetops and the
hedgerows. I wound my window up a little. "I delivered some
stuff to your office Friday. You weren't about."

She glanced at me quickly then looked back at the
darkening sky. "Oh. I quit."

"What?"

"My job. I quit my job."

"Why?"

She shrugged and kept her face turned away. "Dunno.
Bored."

I brushed imaginary crumbs from my trousers. "You
could've told me, Helen."

She shrugged again. "Doesn't matter."

I looked at the sky. After a while I said, "What'll you do?"

"Don't know. Something'll turn up. Mum can support me
for a while. Dad left her well provided for. He got that right,
at least."

I shook my head. "For fuck's sake, Helen."

I felt her eyes on my face. "What?"

"I haven't got the first idea where I stand with you." I felt the sulleness in my voice, hated it.

"How is this suddenly about you?" She spoke mildly. "We've been together, what, six months? We get on well, we have a good time. I don't see the problem."

I still wouldn't look at her. "No. I know you don't."

She started the engine. "Come on. Let's go to mine. We'll have some ice cream then I'll shag your brains out. How does that sound?"

"Don't patronise me," I said.

"Why not?" she said. "You know you love it." As she turned onto the main road the first drops of rain snapped off the windscreen like gunshots.

We were sharing a tub of Haagen Daz Praline and Cream when her mother called. Helen took the phone into the kitchen, opened a bottle of Becks, drank it as she spoke.

When the call ended she came back into the living room. Her smile was fixed, her eyes too bright.

"Everything OK?" I said.

"Fine, fine." She put the empty bottle on the coffee table.

"Perhaps I'll get to meet your mother one day."

"Oh, yes," she said. "One day." She put her arms around my neck and pulled me to her.

When we kissed she tasted of ice cream and beer and cigarettes. I felt something turn inside me. I wanted to pull away from her, but I couldn't.

*

Mid-morning I walk to Corrigan's office behind the scrapyard on Old Palace Street. The door to the stained Portakabin is half-open. Corrigan sits behind a cluttered desk, a file open in front of him, a biro clenched between his teeth. He looks up, beckons me inside, gestures towards the chair opposite his desk. I clear a handful of Lever-arch files from the chair and sit down. The office is cool enough, but it smells of cigar smoke and old sweat.

Corrigan is in his fifties, with thinning, sandy hair swept back. There's sweat on his forehead and on his heavy jowls. His shoulders are broad and his stomach swells over the waistband of his trousers. He wears braces and a candy-stripe shirt that's open at the neck.

He takes the biro from his mouth, examines the chewed end, tosses it onto the desk. "What?" His eyes narrow as he looks at me.

"Got anything for me?" I'm sucking an extra strong mint. I feel sick and my head aches.

"Had something Thursday. As you know. Where were you, Mike?"

I look at my hands. The chair creaks as I lean forward.

"Something came up."

"Right." Corrigan looks at the ceiling, puffs the air from his cheeks. "And now you're broke, need some drinking money."

"Have you got anything?"

He sighs, snaps open a drawer, fishes out a handful of computer printouts. "Here. Mostly Bowthorpe, the Larkman, Mile Cross. Some of these haven't paid for weeks."

"The Larkman. Great."

He shrugs. "What do you expect? So you're left with the shit, whose fault is that?"

"Any chance of a sub?"

He starts to laugh, then says, "You're serious? Fuck, no. I'm here until six. Catch me before that and you'll get your cut. If I don't see you I'll send Ken round. And you know how thorough Ken is."

"I know the score, Corrigan."

"Mr Corrigan," he says, absently. He's looking at the papers again, I'm already forgotten.

At about noon I knock on the front door of a run-down council house on the Bowthorpe estate. The small front lawn is overgrown. A tiny, pink tricycle and a rusting, crimson scooter lurk in the undergrowth.

The day is clear and hot. I can feel the sweat in my hair and my cotton shirt seems molded to my back. I smell my odour, oozing up from my chest and armpits. I pop a mint into my mouth, crunch it immediately.

The door opens and a young woman with lank, brown hair, wearing a stained white T-shirt and black leggings, looks at me. "Mrs Harrison?" I say.

Her shoulders slump. "Oh shit," she says.

Inside the house is tidier than I expect. The living room is small, undecorated, sparsely furnished, smells of cigarettes and soiled nappies. Mrs Harrison stands with her arms folded, shaking her head. "I haven't got it." Her voice is high and wavering.

I sigh and look at the papers that Corrigan gave me. "That's what you told my colleague last week, apparently. With interest, I need a hundred. Now."

She throws her hands in the air. "Or what? You gonna start taking stuff? Help yourself." She looked around the room, at the old TV and video in the corner.

"What about your husband? Perhaps we could have a word with him?" I try to sound menacing, but my heart's not in it. I'm tall, heavily built, but I haven't hit anyone since I was at school.

She lights a cigarette. "If you can find him, you can ask him. It's his debt, anyway. You can take it out of the useless shite's hide for all I care."

There's a noise by the door and a little girl peeps at us from the other room. She's perhaps two years old with wide, almond-brown eyes. When she sees me she smiles shyly and I smile back. "Hayley, go to your room. I told you to stay in your fucking room." The little girl looks at her mother, flinching at the anger in her voice. Her face crumples.

"There's no need…" I begin to say as she starts to cry, but her mother pushes the door shut and turns on me.

"Mind your own fucking business." Her eyes are vacant, her face pinched and defeated.

I look at the floor. "Right. Money. I need to take something with me."

She blows a thin stream of smoke through pursed lips. She looks at me. "Take me," she says.

"What?"

"Don't look so innocent." She points at the worn settee. "We can do it on there. Or have a quick one upstairs. I'm not fussy. And we're talking about a ton, aren't we? I suppose I'd better go down on you for that." There's a sneer on her face and in her voice. Her face is tilted upwards as she looks at me.

I shake my head. I reach for the door. Without looking at her I say, "Someone'll be back next week."

As I fumble my way outside she doesn't speak, just watches me, her expression blank. Outside I wipe the sweat from my face. I walk awkwardly down the path, trying to conceal my erection. I can still hear the child's cries. The house is out of sight before they fade away.

*

"I was a drunk for four years, give or take," I said. I was lying on my back on Helen's bed, letting my breathing settle, watching the patterns the sunlight made on the ceiling as it angled through the thin curtains.

She lay close to me, her body sweat-slick against mine, her arm across my stomach. I could smell her perfume and her hair and feel my heart hammering in my chest.

"I didn't say anything," she said. Her voice was drowsy, muffled, her mouth against my skin.

"You always do after we make love," I said, "I thought I'd pre-empt you. I've been sober two years, since I was twenty-eight. I don't know why I started drinking, I don't know why I stopped. My dad left when I was two. Mum died when I was sixteen. I lived with an uncle for a while, then I moved out and I've lived alone ever since. Which is fine. No secrets, no skeletons. I just lost it for a while, that's all."

She looked up at me. Her hair was wild, her eyes wide, her mouth half-open. "What's the matter, Mike?"

"Nothing."

"Could've fooled me. You don't have to tell me any of this."

"Really?"

She moved the palm of her hand across my flat stomach. I closed my eyes. "We've had such a nice time. Don't spoil it."

"Helen, I don't know you. Your family, your past." I put my hand on her head. "You won't tell me anything."

She flicked her tongue across my nipple. "It's boring. Anyway, you don't need to know, or understand. Just accept."

"And you accept me, do you?"

She looked up, surprise on her face. "Yes. Of course."

I hesitated. "Marry me, then."

"Oh fuck," she said. She buried her face in my stomach, then lifted it up again. "Where did that come from?"

"It's not so unreasonable, is it? We've been courting eighteen months."

"Courting?" She said. She sat up, shook her head, looked at the window. "Courting. Is that what we've been doing?" I stared at the profile of her small breasts, the curve of her back. The sunlight through the curtains illuminated the fair hairs on her skin, blurring her outline. I wanted to pull her to me again, but I didn't.

"That's a no then, is it?" I said.

She lit a cigarette, fiddled with the nail on her big toe. "If it's not broken, don't fix it."

"How about if one of us thinks it's broken and the other doesn't?"

She turned her head slowly, looked into my face. "Then we've got a problem."

I nodded. I felt sick. We were quiet for a moment, then Helen said, "By the way, mum can't make it tonight."

"Surprise, surprise."

"It's not her fault. She's got issues."

"Are we still going, then?" I was surprised by the adolescent sulleness in my voice. "All things considered."

"Of course," she said brightly. "A posh dinner. You're buying. Of course we're going." Her smile was off-centre.

That evening we ate at Green's restaurant on Lower St Giles. Helen wore a short white dress, strappy high-heeled shoes and more jewellery and make-up than usual. She bristled with an odd, unfocused energy. She drank red wine with her meal, brandy afterwards. Nothing I ate or drank had any flavour. All evening her lips were red and wet. All evening I looked at them and wondered how they'd taste.

*

It's gone eight before I make it to The Yellow Rose. As I push the bar door open it occurs to me that I've gone nine hours without a drink. Far too long. I clap my hands, rub them together. "Right," I say to Trish as I approach the bar. "The usual, please. This is an emergency." She has her back to me and turns slowly. Her face is white and her eyes are wet. "What?" I say.

"I've been trying to reach you."

I try to smile. "What?" I say again. That something's wrong is obvious even to me, and I'm curious and everything, but most of all, I want my drink.

"It's Lenny. He's dead."

I look at the fresh tears on her face, the redness around her eyes. My God, I think, she really cares. "Shit," I say, "better make it a double."

Later, at my flat, when we can talk, Trish says, "His neighbour found him this morning. He always takes his Sunday papers round. Heart attack, it looks like. Dead in his chair."

I rub my eyes. The booze has taken a long time to work this evening. "Poor Lenny," I say.

"He's got an ex-wife somewhere, hasn't he? And a couple of grown up daughters."

"I think so. I'm not sure." I frown and give a short laugh. "I don't even know his surname."

"Yes you do," Trish says.

"I do?"

"Yes. It's Coleman. He told you."

"Did he?" I shrug. "I don't remember."

"Oh, Mike," Trish says softly. She blows on her coffee, sips it carefully, looks at the floor.

It's almost one before she leaves. She hesitates by the door.

"Have you eaten?" she says. She brushes something off my shoulder, briefly touches my cheek.

"I had lunch."

She raises an eyebrow. "Which was?"

I let my shoulders slump. "A Mars Bar."

"Bloody hell, Mike."

"A King Size Mars Bar."

She looks at me, her face pinched with concern. She folds her arms across her chest. She wears blue jeans and a thin, lemon-coloured sweater. She's attractive and sweet and she cares about me. I look back at her and feel nothing. "Mike. You'll end up like Lenny. You know that, don't you?"

"Well, thanks for that, Trish. That's helped a lot."

She shakes her head, pushes her hair away from her eyes. Then her expression sharpens and she says, "Something's happened, hasn't it?"

"Well, yes. I mean, Lenny..."

"No. Something else."

I let out a breath. "There's been a couple of phone calls, that's all. Perhaps four, five at the most."

"What sort of calls?"

"Silent ones. I tried 1471. Number withheld."

"Helen."

"I don't know who else it could be."

"Bastard."

"But we mustn't jump to conclusions."

"Fucking Helen. You'd think she'd done enough damage."

"It's probably nothing."

She looks at me again and her expression changes. "You hope it is her, don't you?"

I shrug, try to laugh, "God, no. I..."

"It doesn't matter. None of my business." She looks at my chest. When she kisses my cheek her lips are cold. "Take care," she says. She shuts the door behind her before I can reply.

I stare at the handle and smell her perfume. I bite my lip so hard that I taste blood.

*

The man at my front door was short, in his fifties, smartly dressed in a dark suit with a white shirt and a burgundy silk tie. There were patches of grey in his short hair and in his neatly trimmed beard. It was a Saturday afternoon and I'd fallen asleep in front of the TV. I rubbed my eyes and looked at him. "Can I help you?"

"It's Mike, isn't it?" he said. He held his head to one side and didn't quite meet my eyes.

I nodded.

He bit his lip. "I'm sorry to disturb you. You don't know me. My name is Peter Sims. I'm Helen's father."

My mouth hung open. He stroked his beard. After a moment he said, "Can I come in?" I waved him through without speaking.

"It's not the first time," he said. I passed him a cup of coffee and turned the TV off.

"What do you mean?" I said.

"It's not the first time Helen's claimed that I'm dead. And her mother too, actually." He tried to smile. "Perhaps we should take the hint."

"I don't understand any of this."

"And why should you?" He sighed, sat back in the chair. "I'm sorry, son. If I'd known earlier I would've got in touch, I swear I would."

"Please. Don't call me son. My dad left before I knew him." I felt my cheeks colour. "It sounds silly, but..."

"No problem. I'm sorry, Mike."

"Anyway, Helen and I have been together nearly two years."

"That long? My God." He touched his beard again. His fingers were slim, his nails neatly manicured. "She lives alone, we don't see that much of her. And it's been a while since...well, we thought she was better."

"Better?"

He loosened his tie. "The lies, the stories, the bloody fantasy world she lives in. It's our fault. Her mother and I. She's an only child, you see, we...indulged her." He saw the expression on my face. "Let me come at this another way." He was quiet for a moment. "Mike, you had a drink problem, I believe?"

I smiled thinly. "I'm a sober alcoholic, if that's what you mean."

"Yes. And she told you that I drank, that booze killed me, effectively."

"Something like that."

"I expect she drank quite heavily around you."

I nodded and looked at my hands.

He rubbed his eyes. "The last relationship she had, before you, was about three years ago. His name was Adam. He was an ex-junkie, clean for two years. Helen told him her younger sister died from a heroin overdose."

"Her sister?"

"She's never had a sister, Mike." He looked at the wall. "It gets worse. She told him she was an addict, too. That she needed his help." He shook his head. "We thought she probably smoked some cannabis with her college friends. Who the hell doesn't? But heroin? So she started injecting. She was on the stuff until the relationship ended. Then she stopped." He clicked his fingers. "Just like that."

"What happened to Adam?"

"He started using again. He died in a squat a year ago. Took some stuff that was too pure for him, apparently." I looked at him. His face was bleak, his eyes empty. "That's not all." He closed his eyes, opened them again. "Before that it was an older man. A rehabilitated sex offender."

"Jesus Christ."

"She told him I'd abused her since she was eight years old. He believed her. She told him all the details. She said he liked that."

"What happened?"

"She got bored, as usual. He left the area suddenly. God knows where he is now."

"She needs help. Or locking up."

He nodded slowly, not really listening. "There were others. A compulsive gambler, a shop lifter." He shrugged. "We always forgave her. And we thought she was over it."

"How did you find out about us?"

"Helen told me." There were lines under his eyes, I noticed, and a sallowness to his skin. "You asked her to marry you?"

I nodded. "Perhaps, in retrospect, a mistake."

"On the contrary," he said quickly. "You put her off. You should thank God for that. Are you still sober, Mike?"

I nodded.

"Then count your blessings," he said. He put his face in his hands then looked up at me. His eyes were dark, his pupils had shrunk to the size of pinpricks.

After he'd gone I stood in the kitchen with my hands in my pockets and gazed out at the bland autumn day. Then I put my jacket on and walked to the corner shop and bought a litre of Bell's whisky. Back in my flat I tore off the lid and sucked at the bottle like a baby desperate for it's mother's milk. I closed my eyes as it burnt its way down. I wondered why the hell I'd left it so long.

*

It's Wednesday lunchtime before I see Trish again. The heat broke overnight; I'd listened to the rain thrash and hiss against the hot road outside my bedroom window. I smelled the warm night smells that the rain released. And I sweated. But that had nothing to do with the temperature.

"You look like shit," Trish says. She looks sweet in a collarless white blouse, with her hair up.

"Why, thank you."

"The usual?" She tilts her dark eyes up at me, keeps her expression neutral.

"No." I put my hands on the bar to stop them shaking. "No, I'll have a coke."

She folds her arms. "Are you taking the piss?"

"No. I haven't had a drink since Sunday." I smile. "It feels fucking awful. And it'll get worse. But then it'll get better."

She looks at me for a while. "Are you doing this for Helen?"

"No. I'm doing it for me." Trish nods, serves me my coke. I take a sip. It's cold and sweet and it makes my teeth ache. "After your shift can we walk into town, have a coffee or something?"

She nods again, slowly. "Have you had any more calls?"

I sip my coke again and look at my hands.

*

I knocked on Helen's door for twenty minutes before she answered. It was Sunday lunchtime, a week after her father's visit. She answered the door in her pink towelling dressing gown. There were dark patches under her eyes and her hair was dishevelled.

She wrinkled her nose. "God, you stink of booze."

"Nice to see you too, Helen."

"What do you want?" She shivered slightly. The day was overcast and a cold wind kept the temperature down.

I shrugged. "You don't ring, you don't write. What's a boy to think?"

She frowned. "You're pissed, aren't you?"

"Can I come in?"

She hesitated, then her shoulders slumped. "Just for a minute. I suppose I owe you that."

As I brushed past her I put my hand on her waist and she turned her face away from mine.

We sat at the table in Helen's kitchen. She poured herself some mineral water and lit a cigarette. "I am sorry," she said. "If that's any consolation."

I nodded, ran a finger along the grain of the table. "I still love you."

"For fuck's sake, Mike."

"What's the big deal? You've told a few fibs. Nothing we can't work through."

"Mike, what colour is the sky on your planet? There is no 'us'. There never was, really."

"I imagined it all, did I?" She said nothing, just sipped her water and stared at the tip of her cigarette. "Your father seems like a nice man," I said.

She looked at me then and smiled. "That's what everyone says. Perhaps they're right. Stranger things have happened."

"What's this? Do I sense family secrets? Skeletons in cupboards?"

She screwed up her face, thought for a moment. "Poor little rich girl, that's me. I've always had whatever I wanted. My mother called me a spoilt bitch once, and you know what they say, it takes one to know one." She looked at me and smiled oddly. "It's just that I've got all these empty spaces where my feelings should be. Like you once said about yourself, Mike; I'm just a fuck up."

"We do it to ourselves," I said. "To paraphrase Radiohead."

Helen stubbed out her cigarette and gazed at a spot on the wall, her eyes wistful and distant. "I wish he was dead. I wish they both were." She blinked once, slowly, shook her head, looked at me. "Oh, Mike. You still here? Look, you'd better go." She spoke softly. She touched the back of my hand. "Call me when you're sober."

*

Trish and I sit at a window seat in Oliver's, eating bacon rolls and drinking frothy coffee. There's a smear of ketchup on her upper lip and she licks it off deftly. I push half of my roll to one side.

"What's up?" Trish says.

"Nothing. Just full, that's all."

"Come round mine later. I'll cook you something."

"That'd be nice."

"Right," Trish says and wipes her hand across her mouth. Outside the wind picks up and the clouds are lower and darker. "About those phone calls?"

I look at a sandwich container and a crisp packet as they skitter past the window. "Yes. Very odd."

"Odd?"

I shift in my seat and look her. "Helen phoned me on Monday. In the afternoon, I think it was. I was in bad way, it was hard to tell."

"You're sure it was Helen?"

"Yes. She spoke. She said, "You're sober, aren't you, Mike?" Well, I suppose I was. Technically. I put the phone down. Somehow I got through the rest of the day and, later, I wondered if I'd dreamt it. I had lots of dreams on Monday. About the dad I never met. About mum." I hesitate. "About you, actually." I felt her eyes on my face. "Then Helen called me again yesterday."

"What did she want?"

"Me. Apparently. She sounded faintly hysterical. I think she was drunk." I finish my coffee. It's darker than ever outside the window. "She said she'd been waiting for me. That I was ready for her now and she was ready for me."

"What the bloody hell was she talking about?"

I laugh. "She told me that she'd just killed her parents."

"Christ, Mike."

"I told her to call the Samaritan's. To get herself some help. Then I put the phone down."

"And that was that?"

"Yes."

"She didn't call again? You didn't phone her back, make sure her parents were OK?"

"No. She's a sad little fantasist, Trish."

She sighs, leans forward, puts her elbows on the table. "I know. Poor Helen. I almost feel sorry for her."

"Almost." I touch her arm. "But she's not our problem, Trish."

She smiles. We both jump as the first rain clatters against the window.

Time Bleeds

1.

She was in her mid-fifties, I suppose. Very prim. Austere, even. Dark hair, flecked with grey, scraped back into a tight bun. An ivory-coloured blouse, buttoned at the sleeve and throat and a pleated, below-knee length dark woollen skirt. Black tights. Sensible shoes. Spectacles. She sat in a corner of the dentist's waiting room and I gave her a brief, meaningless smile as I entered then took a seat in the opposite corner. Apart from us the room was empty and the silence was awkward. I hate waiting rooms. After them the dentist's chair is almost a relief.

She caught my glance and I cleared my throat and stared at the watercolour print on the wall next to me. It was a view of Norwich cathedral. Most original.

I heard a rustle and glanced at my companion again as she put the magazine she was reading back on the table. Then she folded her hands in her lap and said, "You should ask her out."

After a moment I said, "What?"

"Becky. You should ask her out. You'd be pleasantly surprised." Her voice was a conversational monotone. She stared at the empty chair opposite her as she spoke.

"Do I know you?" I said.

"The age difference bothers you," she said. A pause, then, "No, that's not quite right. You think that it will bother her. It won't. Just the opposite. She likes you very much. You could be good together." Another pause. "A good...fit. But you must be brave. Take a chance. You'll be rewarded."

When I was sure she'd finished I said, "You're a friend of Becky's, then? Or this is some sort of joke? I don't…"

The intercom cut me off. It called Judy Byatt to Dr Calder's room. It startled me into silence. Across the room Judy Byatt's hands clutched the arms of her chair and she sat upright and looked at me as though seeing me for the first time.

She smiled and said, "Goodness. That made me jump. I must have dropped off." Then she stood, smoothed her skirt over the backs of her thighs and left.

A little later I had a couple of back teeth filled under a local anaesthetic. I'm not sure I needed it, though. I'm not sure I'd have felt anything anyway.

The next day, at work, Becky brought me a cup of coffee at ten-thirty. "Your turn, I think," she said, clunking the mug onto my desk, "but a girl could die of thirst waiting for you."

"Sorry," I said.

"I cleaned your mug as well. I think I wiped out at least three new life forms in the process."

"What can I say? I'm a busy man. Time is money and all that."

We both looked at the Word document open on my PC screen. A report on a site investigation at a building site just outside Dereham. Fascinating stuff. Becky peered closer. "Hold on, you lazy sod. You haven't done anything. You're still on the summary, same as before you went to the dentist yesterday."

"Tangibly, I haven't done anything," I said, "but I've been thinking really, really hard. Pretty deep stuff. Can't expect a slip of a girl like you to understand."

She cuffed my head gently. "Cheeky bastard."

I quickly checked our medium sized, open plan office for any sign of my boss, before closing Word and checking my e-mails. Becky moved closer still and her arm touched my shoulder. She wore some kind of fruity, summery scent and I tried not to breathe it in too deeply.

"That's an interesting e-mail," she said, pointing at the screen. "Increase the size of your penis. Open that one."

I deleted my junk mail rapidly. "Entirely unsolicited, I assure you."

"I'll take your word for it," she said.

Becky was twenty-two. I was forty. Her fiancé, and childhood sweetheart, had ended their engagement a couple of months earlier. I'd spent the last three years piecing together the remnants of my ego after my wife had left me for my former best friend.

Becky was radiant. And she didn't seem to realise it, which made her even more radiant in my eyes. She had short blond hair, parted in the middle. A dusting of understated freckles. Blue eyes. An easy smile. White teeth. Snub nose. All delectably arranged. I yearned for her hopelessly, silently. My heart twisted at the sound of her voice or the smell of her perfume as she approached my desk. I felt like a pathetic old fool.

Just before twelve-thirty she came to see me again. "What are you doing for lunch?"

"I was going to work through," I said, "thus exhibiting my undying commitment to the company."

"Ok. I'm walking into town. Going to wander around some bookshops. Want to come?"

"Sounds good to me," I said.

It was an anonymous spring day. No wind. A little sun. Some random, half-hearted cloud. The air tasted and smelled of nothing.

"How did you get on at the dentist?" she said.

"Why?" I looked at her face. Her expression was guileless. "It's a simple enough question."

"Great," I said, "it cost me thirty quid to be injected and prodded and drilled."

"What's up, Cam? You seem a bit odd."

"I'm always odd."

"That's a very good point. But, no. Odder still."

I shrugged. "Dunno. Must be my age. Maybe it's the menopause. Or Alzheimer's."

There must have been something in my voice. I felt her look at me. "Don't be silly."

"Anyway," I said, "how's Steve."

We were opposite Ottaker's now. When Becky spoke her voice was small and cold. "Steve's history. I don't talk about Steve. You know that, Cameron."

"Just showing concern, that's all. Being a friend."

I stared at the display in Ottaker's window. I felt her eyes on my face. "No you're not. I don't know what you're doing. Shall I ask you about Sarah?"

"Be my guest. Sarah's fine. Better than fine. Last I heard she was three months pregnant."

"Shit. Really?" I nodded. "Cameron, I'm so sorry."

I closed my eyes and leant my forehead against the window. "No. I'm sorry." I said shit and bollocks a few times. I congratulated myself on my literacy and intelligence. "Just ignore me. Or shoot me. Or both. I'm just a silly old sod."

"Not so much of the old," Becky said. "We'll agree on silly sod for now."

"Cheers," I said.

A little later we sat upstairs in the Starbuck's next to Norwich market. Becky sipped her hot chocolate then tongued a line of whipped cream from her top lip. "How long have you known?"

"About a week," I said. "Sarah phoned me. Said she didn't want me to hear from anyone else."

"That's nice of her."

"I think she meant it. She seems to have mellowed."

"Or maybe she feels guilty. You wanted kids so badly and she said she didn't. Even Sarah's got to realise how much this will hurt you."

"Actually, I'm fine about it. I wish them well. I told her so. I think she thought I was taking the piss but I wasn't. People change, that's all. She shouldn't feel guilty."

She looked at me for a moment, her expression neutral. "That's such bollocks, Cameron. I mean, top marks for the stiff upper lip, but cut the crap. It hurts. You're upset. It's allowed, you know."

"I'm not upset. Not about Sarah."

"And when the baby's born?"

"Too far ahead to worry about. Her and David are talking about moving, anyway. Manchester. He's been offered a job there."

"Out of sight out of mind?"

"Something like that."

"Speaking of which," she said. She cradled her mug in both hands and chewed her lip.

"What?"

"I've handed in my notice." She offered me a quick smile. "I'm going back to college. With a bit of help from mum and dad. Time I stopped pissing about and thought about a career."

"I see."

"I would have said something earlier, but.."

"That's ok. It's good. I'm pleased for you."

"Right."

"Shit. Look at the time. We'd better be getting back."

I stood but she remained sitting. She tipped her head to one side and smiled at me. Her freckles darkened slightly when she smiled and deep dimples formed in her cheeks. "Do you ever say what you really think?"

"What?"

Becky stood quickly, still smiling and reached a hand out and touched my cheek in an odd, tender gesture and I blinked twice, rapidly. "Nothing. Nothing at all. Come on. Let's get back to the shit-hole."

I followed her down the steep stairway and out into the feeble sunlight.

We were quiet on the way back to the office. Eventually I said, "We're friends, though, right? We can still meet up after you've left. Lunch and stuff."

She half-laughed. "No," she said, "we can't." She shook her head. "Friends, indeed."

Stung, I turned towards her. "What the hell is that supposed to mean? I don't get you, Becky."

"I know you don't. We're not friends. Lunch?" She sneered around the word. "Is that what you want? Coffee once a month? Fill me in on the office gossip? No thanks." I felt my cheeks redden. We walked in silence for a minute then Becky said, "And don't sulk. It doesn't suit you."

"I'm not sulking. I don't know what to say."

"How do you feel, what do you want? So you've been hurt. Stop hiding behind it."

"For fucks sake, Becky."

"What? And by the way. I leave tomorrow."

"Tomorrow?"

"Yes. It's Friday. I'm admin, remember. Unimportant. Only had to give a weeks notice."

The office was approaching fast. "Come out with me then. Sometime."

"Out? Out where?"

"I don't know. The cinema? A meal?"

"Lunch, you mean? As friends?"

"If you like.."

"Cameron! Fuck lunch. Just say it. Last chance."

We were at the glass doors that led to our office. She went to open them but I stopped her. "Ok. A date? Is that what you want to hear? You can wear a nice dress. Maybe I'll splash out on a new shirt and some aftershave. And there'll be that awkward bit at the end of the evening when I won't know whether to kiss you or not." I had my hand on her arm. I pulled it away.

"That's it exactly. Well done. And I'm free this Saturday. Thanks for asking." She was beaming at me.

"You sadistic bastard," I said.

"Now you're getting it," she said.

I touched her arm again. "But you mean it? About Saturday?"

"Of course I do."

I grimaced. "But the age difference. Doesn't it bother you?"

She laughed. "Have you listened to yourself recently? What bloody age difference."

"Just don't say the "S" word," Stuart said.
"What?" I said.
"Soulmates," Stuart said. "If you say you and Becky are soulmates I'll throw up, I swear I will."
"You're just jealous," I said. It was a month after I first asked Becky out and Stuart and I were on the Riverside development, in one of the glitzy, soulless new pubs that he liked.
"I don't think Becky's quite my type, love."
"Well, no. But as we've been here for an hour and you haven't mentioned Jason yet, I'm guessing he's blown you out."
Stuart sighed theatrically. "Unfortunate choice of words, but yes. He left a week ago, just after we got back from Portugal. Bastard. Made sure he got his holiday first."
"I'm sorry."
A small shrug. "Don't be. He was never my soulmate, that's for sure. Plenty more fish and all that." Stuart sipped a coke. He was a few years older than me but looked younger. He was tanned and slender with black hair cut very short. He wore a collar-less white shirt and black jeans. "So. You and Becky. The real thing, is it? Do I get to be a bridesmaid at last?"
I looked into my beer. Stuart was being particularly camp this evening and it made me uncomfortable. I had no idea why it did and I would never have admitted it to him. "It's a little early for that, I think."
"Still. I've never seen you so happy."
"No. Me neither. It's very odd."
"Try just relaxing and enjoying it." He arched his eyebrows. "And yes, I do say that to all the boys." At a nearby table a young couple glanced at us and sniggered. I drank most of my pint in a single swallow and said nothing. "I'm not embarrassing you, am I, Cameron?"
"Of course not," I said. Stuart smiled and fished a slice of lemon from his drink and dropped it into an ashtray. I leant forward. "You don't think it's creepy, do you? The age difference?"
He rolled his eyes. "Jesus Christ. Not this again."
"But she could be my daughter."
"But the point is, she isn't. It will only be a problem if you let it. Which I suspect you will. I think you're allergic to being happy."

"I wish I hadn't asked."

"So do I, my dear. So do I." He sipped his coke, seemed to savour it. "You know, I've been dry more than ten years but sometimes I can still taste the Jack Daniels."

"Do you miss it?"

"Every day." He gave a wry grin. "Don't miss the blackouts, though. Or the lost weekends." He raised his glass. "A toast. To you and Becky." I drained my pint obediently.

"And that mad old woman at the dentist who started it all," I said.

He grunted. "I rather hoped you'd forgotten that."

"Why? Don't you believe me?"

"It's not that. I don't like the thought of my best friend being delusional."

"I didn't imagine it."

"Of course not. I expect she's a serial matchmaker. Goes from waiting room to waiting room, putting people together. Pity you didn't get a card. I might have given her a call."

"I know how it sounds."

"I doubt that you do. But just forget it, Cam. It's not important. The way you tell it, you and Becky would have got together anyway."

"I suppose you're right."

"Of course I'm right." He grinned and slid his glass towards me. Raising his voice, he said, "now shut up and get your Auntie Stuart a drink."

I fetched our drinks and went to the toilet. As I pissed mindlessly a tall, powerfully built man wearing cream-coloured chinos and a black t-shirt stood a couple of feet to my left and started to do the same. I finished what I was doing and tucked myself away. I gave my companion a tentative glance. He'd finished as well, apparently, but he stood with his cock out, his arms at his side, staring at the white tiles in front of him. Then the air around him changed and I knew what was coming. "You're very ungrateful," he said. I recognised the voice, the monotone.

I sighed. "What?" I said.

"I understand denial," he said, "especially when it's encouraged by foolish friends. It serves no purpose, though. Best go through life with your eyes open, Cameron. Don't you think?"

I washed my hands and splashed cold water over my face. In the mirror above the wash-basin I could see the t-shirted

man in profile. He was motionless still and a thin line of drool
hung from his mouth. I turned away from the mirror. "Yes. You
helped very much. I appreciate it. Becky and I are very happy.
Thank you." Afterwards, thinking back to what I said, it seemed
absurd. It didn't at the time. I was humouring him. I didn't
know what else to do.

"Oh dear," the man said. "You still doubt. Very well."
He was quiet for a while but I knew he hadn't finished. There
was still a tension in the air, an electricity; something like
the feeling you get just before a storm. Eventually, "Your
friend. Stuart." For the first time the monotone broke
slightly. As he said my friend's name I sensed a hint of
contempt. "His mother will die a week next Thursday. In the
afternoon. I could give the time, to the second, but that seems
unnecessary."

"That's not funny," I said, then the man stirred, shook
his head, glanced down in bewilderment at his exposed cock. The
door to the toilets opened and two half-pissed youngsters
almost fell through it. I grabbed it before it closed and left,
hoping they didn't see the expression on my face.

"You took your time," Stuart said. "Did you get lucky
or something." Then, "Shit, are you ok? Your face is white. I
mean even whiter than normal. Sit down before you fall down."

I did as he said. I looked at my pint of lager and pushed
it away. "Don't feel too great, now you come to mention it.
Something I ate, perhaps."

"It came on bloody quickly, mate." The campness had gone
and I was touched by the concern on his face. "No pizza and a
movie for us tonight, I fear."

"I think not. Sorry."

"Hey, I'm used to being stood up. Will you stay with
Becky tonight?"

"No. I'll have a night on my own."

"God, you must be ill. You'll be ok, though?"

"Of course. Don't fuss."

"Come on, let's get you a taxi before you throw up."

I let him lead me outside. The air was warm and sweet
as dusk fell and I felt a little better. I followed Stuart
towards the taxi rank then drew alongside him. "How's your mum?"
I said, as casually as I could.

"My mum?"

I shrugged. "Yeah. Just wondered."

"She's still a bitch. Other than that she's fine. Thanks

for asking." His eyes narrowed. "Why, though? Let's try and remember the last time you asked about my mother. That's right. Never."

"I've been thinking about mine, that's all. Things I wished I'd said, stuff like that." I struggled not to blush at the lie. "No offence meant."

"Of course not. You just threw me, that's all." He laughed. "Actually, she's a bloody embarrassment. I've lost count of the men she's been through since dad died. And it's me that's let the family down."

"I'm sorry, Stuart."

A black cab pulled up to the taxi rank and Stuart hailed it. "Don't be silly. Give Becky a kiss from me. No tongues, though. I've got my reputation to think of."

He walked back towards the pub. The taxi driver gave me a look and I shrugged and climbed into the back of his cab.

There was a storm the day Stuart's mother died. I was at work and I saw the thunderhead approaching through the large window next to my desk. The first crack of thunder sounded just before noon. It was loud enough to make every head in the office turn. The sky was plum-coloured, heavy with cloud. I watched the first bolt of lightening, ragged and melodramatic. Then the rain came; torrential, apocalyptic almost. I thought of Becky, temping somewhere across the other side of the city, and of how utterly mundane the office seemed without her. I didn't think of Stuart's mother. I'd put her firmly out of my mind; dismissed the incident in the pub toilet as a delusion borne of an imminent fever.

Yet when the personal call was put through to me just after two that afternoon, as the rain was clearing and thin sunshine was filtering through the retreating cloud, I knew instantly who it was.

Stuart's flat was pristine as always. Every surface polished, the carpets immaculately hoovered, no magazines or newspapers slung across the arms of chairs or the glass-topped coffee table. Stuart sat neatly in an armchair. I stood and waited for him to say something. Eventually, "Go to the pub, will you? I'll catch up with you later."

"No," I said. "Not yet. Talk to me. You buried your mother this morning. You haven't said a word. Not today, not since…" I let the sentence tail off.

"Perhaps I don't want to talk, Cameron. Have you thought of that?"

"You stayed with me all night when my parents died. Broke a hot date if I remember correctly."

"Well, I'm just a wonderful person, aren't I?"

I ignored the bitterness in his voice. "I'm not leaving you like this."

He sighed. "If you're staying, sit down. You make the room look untidy." The leather sofa squeaked as I sank into it. It was more comfortable than it looked. "She even died stupidly," Stuart said. He loosened his black silk tie and undid his top button. "My father fought cancer for ten years. My mother slipped in the shower and broke her neck. I got to say goodbye to dad. Trust my fucking mother to deny me even that."

His voice broke and he put his head in his hands. I told myself that this was not my fault. That Stuart's mother's death was not related to the message I'd thought I'd received. It was all a stupid coincidence. I couldn't have stopped it. I told myself that again and again.

Later we went to a nearby pub. It was early on a Wednesday evening and we had the bar to ourselves. Stuart sent me to a corner table and fetched the drinks. I hadn't eaten since breakfast and after half a pint I felt light-headed.

"I resent it," Stuart said.

"Resent what?"

"Caring this much. About someone who didn't give a shit about me."

"I'm sure that's not true."

He gave me a look. "Even before she knew I was gay I was never good enough. And she blamed me for dad's illness."

"That's ridiculous."

"Of course it is." He closed his eyes. "Do you know what she said once? I've never told anyone this."

"What?"

He opened his eyes again but didn't look at me. "She said dad had AIDS. The doctors were covering it up. I'd given it to him, of course. Breathing the same air, eating at the same table. She wanted me to move out before I gave it to her."

"Jesus Christ. I'm sorry, Stuart."

He wouldn't meet my eyes. I think he felt he'd said too much. Perhaps that partly explains what happened later. He drained his coke. "Another drink?" he said, pointing at my glass.

"My turn," I said.

"I'll go," he said, and he was at the bar before I could stand.

"Did you know I should have had a brother?" Stuart said a little later. We still had the bar to ourselves. I shook my head. "Stillborn. When I was two, apparently. His name was Brian. I mean, for fuck's sake. Brian. What sort of name is that? I expect mum thought it was my fault she lost the baby. Everything else was my fault, after all. Every-fucking-thing."

His eyes were damp and out of focus. Belatedly, something clicked into place. "Stuart? What's in the glass?"

He gave a tight, humourless grin. "Put it this way. I no longer have to imagine there's Jack Daniel's in my coke."

"Stuart. Ten years. Ten dry years just chucked away."

"Really? Well, who gives a shit?"

"I do. You should."

He snorted and drained his glass. "Tell you what, you get a heck of a hit after ten years." His complexion had changed and his hands were shaking slightly.

I'd known Stuart when he'd been a drunk but never realised the extent of his addiction. He told me the details later, when he was sober. Twice waking up in the Norfolk and Norwich hospital after grand mal seizures. Days, sometimes weeks of his life missing. Mornings spent shaking and dry-heaving until the first shot of vodka or JD snapped the world back in focus. "I can't sit and watch this," I said.

"I'm not asking you to."

"Why, Stuart? I know it's a shock, but you didn't even like your mother."

"No. You're quite right. I hated her, in fact. And everything she stood for. Small-minded prejudice and bigotry. That was her agenda. But it seems I loved her, too. That's the shock. After all she did to me, I still loved her, she can still reduce me to this." He slammed his glass onto the table. An ice-cube spilled out of it and slid onto the floor.
"What sort of person does that make me? That's why I'm drinking. I need it and I deserve it."

He stood and made his way to the bar. "Don't get me one," I said, "I'm not staying."

"Fuck you, then."

"That's all just self-pitying bollocks."

"Thanks, Cameron."

I felt a stab of anger. "We all have skeletons, Stuart. My parents.." I closed my eyes.

Stuart came back to the table. We were both standing now. "What? Come on. Mr Perfect. You never talk about mummy and daddy, do you? What little secrets have you been hiding?"

"Nothing," I said dully.

"Fine," he said. He planted a hand on the back of his chair to steady himself. I tried to remind myself that this wasn't really Stuart at all. "And you knew, didn't you?"

"What?" I said. I felt something lurch in my stomach. Guilt must have radiated from my face.

"A couple of weeks ago, when you asked how mum was. What was that all about? You knew something was going to happen."

"Listen to yourself. She had an accident. How the hell could I have known?"

"Dunno. Call it female intuition. I'm right, though. It's written all over your face."

"It's the drink, that's all. You'll regret this tomorrow."

"Will I? You're the expert now, are you? Get out of my sight. You make me sick." I stood there and looked at my friend.

"Go on. We're through."

"You don't mean that."

He took a step towards me and there was real anger in his eyes. "Don't I? Why do you give a shit, anyway? I only embarrass you. What am I, your token gay friend? Probably scared to turn your back on me. Think I have wet dreams about you, don't you?"

"Stuart."

"Tell you what, if you were the last bloke alive I'd go and have a wank. Sanctimonious prick."

That was all I could take. I stumbled out of the door.

The last I saw of Stuart he was leant against the table, pointing at me, his eyes wide open and staring.

The air was cool and although I'd had little to drink my legs felt weak and my head was spinning. I walked about half a mile, taking no notice of where I was going. I turned a corner and bounced off a large middle-aged man walking a golden Labrador. "Watch it, mate," he said, as his dog yelped and side-stepped inelegantly, hind legs tangling in its lead.

I started to apologise then I saw all expression drop from the man's face and his eyes grow dull and I groaned and said, "No. Not now."

"It's for the best," the man said.

"Leave me alone."

"You don't need the shirt-lifter. It's all for the best." The dog whimpered and tugged at the lead. The voice wasn't entirely a monotone this time. There was a hint of glee;

minuscule, but unmistakable.

I stared at the blank face. "Just fuck off," I said. I ran.

2.

Six months after our first date Becky and I drove to Alnmouth on the Northumberland coast. It was November and the weather was cold and still. On Saturday morning we left our hotel and walked through the village to the beach.

"This was your idea," Becky said. "Just remember that."
She was hunched inside a vast padded jacket.
"You don't like it, then."
"What's to like?" Her scarf covered most of her face, but I could guess at the expression. Pursed lips, pinched cheeks, hooded eyes. After six months Becky no longer seemed quite so radiant.

Miles of beach lay before us. The light was blue-grey, the sea motionless, the sky enormous and unblinking. "I like the bleakness," I said.

"You live in Norfolk, Cameron. How much more bleakness do you need?"

I glanced at her and felt the distance grow between us.
It was a good question.

*

When I first met her parents, after I'd recovered from the shock of them being only five years older than myself, I was struck by their eagerness to accept me. I found it touching at the time and I remember how much it pleased Becky that we all got on. Once, after Sunday lunch, her mother told me how glad she was that Becky had found someone reliable.

"Thanks. I think," I said with a grin.

"Oh, it's definitely a compliment," she said. "After Steve.." her voice tailed off.

We were in the garden. I could see Becky and her father through the kitchen window. They were chatting animatedly and out of earshot. "She never mentions Steve," I said.

"No. Neither do we, I suppose. He mixed with the wrong people. I blame most of her problems on him."

"Problems?"

She blushed and smiled to try and hide it. "You must have noticed her little moods."

"No," I said.

She looked into my face and for a moment she looked much older than forty-five. "You will, Cameron. You will."

A fortnight later, just after we'd made love, Becky said, "You were thinking of her then, weren't you?"

"What?" I was half-dozing. I sat up. Becky had her back to me.

"Sarah. When you came, you were thinking of her. I could tell." Her voice was flat.

"Don't be stupid."

She turned on me. Her teeth were bared. "Stupid? I'll give you fucking stupid." She slapped my face hard. It sounded like a gunshot. Her hand came up and I grabbed it. "You're hurting me," she said. I let go of her hand and she hit me again.

I got out of the bed. "Just go," I said.

"Or what?" Her face was crimson, her eyes wide open.

I could feel the imprint of her hand on my cheek. I was close to tears. "Go," I said.

"Fucking wimp," she said, then her expression slackened and she said, "God. What have I done? I'm so sorry." She put her hands to her face and tears spilled through her fingers. I went to her and she put her head on my chest and cried for twenty minutes.

*

We walked for miles across the sand without speaking. Neither the sea nor the sky seemed capable of movement. The light had an alien quality. Sometimes I forgot that Becky was beside me. All I could hear was the sound of my own breathing and I could taste salt although there was no breeze.

I liked Becky's silences. At least I could pretend they were neutral. Her mood changed abruptly, usually without warning. I learnt to avoid certain subjects; Steve. Sarah. Stuart. Becky's parents. Money. My parent's. But sometimes her face would change anyway, her voice would deepen and an unreadable hatred would flicker in her eyes. And I'd brace myself and wait for it to pass.

At some point, on the way back to our hotel, Becky snaked a gloved hand into my coat pocket. I felt my stomach and shoulder muscles relax. I hadn't realised that I'd been tensing them.

Later, in bed, Becky lay with an arm across my chest. I could smell her perfume and her sweat. "Why do you put up with me?" she said.

I almost said that I had no idea. That was the truth, but it seemed best avoided. "I love you."

"Do you?"

"Yes." I stared at the ceiling. It was nicely artexed and painted the colour of weak coffee.

"Why?"

"There is no why. You either love someone or you don't." My voice was a monotone.

"Do you really believe that?"

"Yes."

"I love you," Becky said.

"Right," I said.

*

Months earlier, after a grim, seemingly endless Bank Holiday weekend, I'd asked Becky if she'd consider seeking professional help.

"Why?" she said. It seemed a strange question. On the Saturday night she'd bitten me twice on the forearm, drawing blood. I wore long-sleeved shirts buttoned to the wrist for a month, waiting for the scars to fade.

"Your temper," I said.

It was Monday evening and Becky was calmer, washed out. I was still wary, though. I was always wary. "You think I need help?" She nodded slowly. "This from the man who receives messages from strangers?"

"That's not fair. I told you, that was all a mistake. False memory. Things got mixed up, that's all."

"I wonder if Stuart sees it that way."

"That's not the point. Stuart's an alcoholic. That distorts everything."

"Does it now?"

"Yes. And stop changing the subject."

"Is that what I'm doing?" she said. She laughed bleakly. "We make a good couple, don't we?"

I looked hard at her. I saw that she meant it.

*

Before she slept Becky ran through her usual check-list. Her mouth was next to my ear. "Have you phoned Sarah today?"

"No."

"Have you thought about her?"

"No."

"How about a while ago? When we were making love? Did you think of her then?"

"No."

"Have you phoned Stuart today?"

"No."

"Good boy," she said. She kissed my cheek. "Night."

She was asleep within minutes. I eased her arm from my chest and she grunted and turned away from me. I went back to staring at the ceiling. It hadn't changed much. I tried to think of Sarah then, but I couldn't. She remained at the back of my mind, along with Stuart and my dead parents. It was getting crowded in there.

I took a walk along the beach in the morning, before breakfast, while Becky slept in. There was some wind now and the sea was dotted with small, foam-flecked waves and occasional clouds gusted across the monochrome sky. I found a coffee shop just down from the front and sat at a corner table. I was the only customer. The air around me changed as the waitress approached me. She was sixteen at most, short and plump, dressed in dark trousers and blouse with a white apron tied around her waist. Her rust-coloured hair was fixed in an off-centre ponytail. She looked at me, eyes vacant, mouth open.

I waited. "You have a message for me, don't you?"

The girl's cheeks flushed pink. "A message? I just want to take your order."

"My order? I'll have a coffee. White, no sugar."

She nodded and turned and shuffled away.

I closed my eyes. "Oh, fuck," I said.

She was back only moments later. I smelled the cigarette smoke and sweat on her clothes. She dumped a mug of coffee onto the table in front of me. "Careful," I said.

"Becky's pregnant," she said, her voice without inflection. "She might keep it. She might not. She hasn't decided yet. She's too scared to tell you."

"Scared?"

"Becky's frightened of you."

"Right," I said.

"As your mother was."

"My mother? And dad as well, I suppose."

"Your father loved you. Despite everything. He was simply a weak man."

"And my mother? Did she love me?"

The girl was quiet. I looked up into her face. She blinked and frowned into the middle distance. Without warning she put her hand on my shoulder. I bit my lip to stop myself screaming. Her nails were bitten to the quick and freckled with specks of purple nail polish.

136

"Your father loved you," she said.

Then the hand was gone and I turned and she was gone, too. I gripped the tabletop to stop my hands shaking. Then I reached for my cup, but it wasn't there. I heard a sound behind me and a moment later the girl was by my side again. She placed a dark green octagonal mug on the table in front of me and filled it with coffee from a stainless steel container. She smelled of Juicy Fruit chewing gum. "I'll bring your milk in a minute," she said. Then she saw my face. "Are you ok?"

"I'm fine," I said. "Fine." I gave her a smile. God knows what it looked like. She backed away from me as one would from a lunatic.

I found a telephone box on the way back to the hotel and, for the first time in six months, dialled Stuart's mobile number. Just as I was expecting the message service to cut in a bleary voice answered. "Do you know what time it is?"

"It's Cameron."

A pause. "Bloody hell. This is a blast from the past. How are you doing?"

"Fine."

"And Becky?"

"Yeah, great. Look.."

"You two tied the knot yet?"

"Not quite. But she's meant to be moving in with me next week."

"That's cute."

I took a breath. "Stuart, I want to apologise."

"Apologise? For what?"

"How we…how we parted. It was my fault. I'm sorry."

"Sorry for what? You got yourself a girlfriend, we drifted apart. These things happen. I'm pretty pre-occupied myself these days. The reason I'm keeping my voice low? Carl here's like a bear with a sore head if he doesn't get his beauty sleep."

"But.." I closed my eyes. "Your mother.."

"My mother? Don't talk about my mother. She only went and re-married. We keep our distance these days. It's best that way." I started to say something then stopped. Stuart said, "You ok, Cameron? Have you been drinking? It's a bit early, isn't it?"

"Is it?" I said. "How about you? Are you dry again?"

"Again? Cheeky sod. I've been dry eleven years next week. Cameron? Are you crying?"

"No."

"Look, call again soon. We'll get together some time. Ok?"

"Yes," I lied. "I'll do that."

I broke the connection. I stepped out of telephone box and faced the beach and the increasingly restless sea and wondered if they were real at all.

*

I was ten when my mother first hit me. It was during a school holiday. It was mid-Summer and stiflingly hot. She stood in the kitchen, smoking a cigarette, staring at the white tiles above the draining board. Her hair was uncombed and she smelt unwashed. Later I found out that this was the beginning of her five-year addiction to prescription painkillers. If someone had told me that at the time it would have meant nothing to me. I was ten and selfish and bored. I can't remember what I said. I wanted to go out, think. Perhaps I was after some money. She sighed and mumbled something. I whined some more. And she hit me in the face.

I remember the shock rather than the pain. And the expression she wore when she hit me again, in the chest and stomach. No expression at all. Her face was blank, her eyes empty. I sat in a corner of the living room for a long while, too stunned to cry. Later my mother helped me up and hugged me and told me she loved me really.

She went to the shop when dad got home and I rushed to his side the instant she was gone and burst into tears and told him everything.

*

As I walked back to the hotel I wondered if Becky was real. Perhaps I'd get back to my room and find it empty except for a single bed. I wasn't sure which option I'd prefer.

But she was there; dressed, arms folded, waiting for me.

*

I loved my father. He was blandly affable, always smiling, ruffling my hair. He took me to football matches and greyhound racing at Great Yarmouth and Swaffham where I'd eat hotdogs and drink Coca-Cola while he bet randomly and almost always lost.

He held me as I cried and I smelled his after-shave and made his shirt wet where I pressed against him. "I'm afraid your mother's not very well," he said eventually.

"Why? Is she going to die?"

"No. But she needs our help. I'm sure she didn't mean to hurt you, Cameron."

"She did, dad," I said. I lifted my shirt and exposed the bruises just below my ribs. "Look." I blinked away fresh tears.

"They'll soon go," he said and his voice seemed suddenly brisker, harder. I'm not sure the bruises registered at all.

"You've got to be brave. This will be our secret. I'll speak to your mother. This won't happen again. You'll see."

I started to say something else, but he was already standing, turning away from me, rubbing his hands together as though cleaning something small and distasteful from his skin.

Two days later she hit me again.

*

"Where have you been?" Becky said.

"Out."

"I've been worried about you."

"Right," I said. But there was something in her voice and I stopped bracing myself and looked into her face. Her expression was one of concern.

"You look awful." She walked up to me and I stiffened. "Are you ill?" she said. She put her arms around my neck and kissed my cheek.

"Actually, I think I might be," I said. I placed my hands on her waist. I glanced over her shoulder at my left arm, looking for the faint scar she'd left there when she'd bitten me three months earlier. The skin was unblemished. I gripped Becky tightly. I clamped my eyes shut and took a deep breath but the tears came anyway.

*

When I turned sixteen the beatings, which had become progressively less frequent during the previous year, stopped completely. My mother received treatment for her addiction and made an almost complete recovery. The three of us lived together, in a state of complete denial, for four more years. Then, one hot Sunday afternoon my parents took a drive to the coast. Dad asked me if I wanted to go but I said I'd stay at home and watch the cricket on TV. While they were getting ready I went into the small, cool garage and drained almost all of the brake fluid from my dad's Austin Allegro. They got as far as the Acle straight before their car left the road, hit a tree head on and exploded.

I made no attempt to hide my guilt and even as the police were telling me of my parents' death I expected my arrest to follow. It never did. Perhaps the car was never examined properly. Perhaps it was too badly damaged. Perhaps I never bled the brake fluid at all.

*

It's dusk and Becky and I are on Alnmouth beach again, hand in hand. We spent the day visiting Dunstanburgh Castle. It was bleak and deserted and Becky loved it.

"We need dogs," she says suddenly.

"We do?"

"Yep. Labradors, I think. At least two. One chocolate, one golden."

She laughs and breaks free of my hand and runs towards the water's edge. The sun is setting gaudily, staining everything pink and crimson.

I think of Stuart. He's an alcoholic. Maybe it's his reality that's altered, not mine.

I watch Becky as she runs. Maybe I'll ask her if she's pregnant later. Maybe not.

My shoulders and back are still tense. I'm waiting for the world to tilt again, for all perspectives to shift once more.

Becky turns and grins at me. Caught by the sunset, her face and hair are the colour of arterial blood.

Simply Dead

"Shit," Vince said.

"My sentiments exactly," I said.

Connelly said nothing. This was understandable under the circumstances. He lay sprawled on his back across the scarred pine coffee table in the middle of the room. There was a small black hole in the centre of his forehead. His open eyes stared up at the ceiling, although I don't suppose he was seeing much. A dark stain had spread across the crotch of his old jeans.

"He's dead, isn't he?" Vince said.

"Not much gets past you, does it?" I said. "I think we can assume he's dead. That or he's learnt to hold his breath for a really long time."

Vince looked at me. He was in his late twenties, the same age as me. He was tall and stooped with long greasy hair and a half-arsed beard. His arms and legs were too long and too thin. He had bad skin and teeth that made you glad he didn't smile much. He was a real hit with the ladies. He was also pretty much my best friend. I didn't want to dwell too much on what that said about me.

"He was your friend, Nick. You should show some respect."

Vince stood by the window of Connelly's bedsit, glancing occasionally through the nicotine stained net curtain at Riverside Road beyond. I was struck again by his gangling ugliness, by the expression of sullen resentment that seemed spot welded to his face.

Respect, I thought. Connelly had been, and for all I knew still was, a drug dealer, a speed addict, a pimp and a paedophile. And they were just his good points. He also had a temper barely this side of psychotic. And until recently he had been my second best friend. Another thought I didn't wish to dwell on. I just shovelled it to the back of my mind with all the other debris. Repression, denial, call it what the fuck you like, it's pretty much essential in my world.

I turned away from Vince and felt better immediately. A bit like turning off a migraine, I suppose.

Connelly's bedsit was even more wrecked than usual. Porn magazines littered the threadbare sofa. The television set, a widescreen Sony that looked too big and too expensive for the room, had been tipped on it's back and disembowelled. A bottle of milk had been smashed in one corner. Clothes and tinned food had been scattered at random. The room stank of sweat and old dope and of Connelly's shit and piss.

"How long had he had this?" I said, kicking the shattered monitor of a Dell 500, the hard disk of which lay next to Connelly's head.

"A couple of months. You'd have known that if you'd bothered to keep in touch."

"I told you. I've been busy."

"What? Those poncy evening classes? You'll be a fucking office slave next." He kicked a beer can and glanced out of the window again. He wore a blue anorak that was short in the arms and too big everywhere else. He sneered across at me. "Still off the drink, are you?"

I ignored him and continued sifting through the debris.

"There's a printer here. And a scanner and a modem." I looked at Vince. "I didn't know Connelly was a nethead."

"There's a lot you don't know, Nick. You're the clever one, you work it out. What would a guy like Connelly find so interesting about the Internet?"

I sifted through a pile of black three and a half-inch disks. "There's got to be a couple of grand's worth here. The computer and the TV."

"So? He could afford it. We all could. I suppose that's why he's dead." He slumped onto the sofa, squashing copies of Color Climax and Rodox. "We're fucked, aren't we, Nick?"

I shrugged.

Vince looked at Connelly and then at me, running his hands through his dirty hair. "You said we'd be safe here, you both did. No fucker will follow us to Norwich, you said."

"Can't be right all the time."

He started to say something else, then glanced at the body again, his nose wrinkling. "God, he stinks," he said. Presumably the stench of Connelly's involuntary bowel movements had finally overcome Vince's own odour.

"He's got a good excuse," I said.

"What is it with you? We're going to be next, aren't we, and you don't seem to give a shit."

I shrugged again.

"It's the Mallon brothers, isn't it?" Vince said. He was sneering now. It rather suited him. "You remember them, Nick. What did you call them? A pair of throwbacks with single figure

IQ's whose Dad should have done us all a favour and settled for a wank? Never find us while they had holes in their arses, you said. Looks like you were wrong, Nick."

"Perhaps," I said, "but maybe it's not the Mallon's. Connelly's not short of enemies, Vince."

"We screwed them out of forty grand, of course it's the fucking Mallon's. What are we going to do, Nick, where are we going to go?"

"We?" I said. "You can do what you like, mate, but I'm going nowhere. I like it here."

"You like Norwich? That figures. Look, we should stick together. You think any of those twats from College will put themselves out for you? You should remember who your friends are."

"It's hard to forget, Vince."

"Whatever. But we can't stay here. I keep expecting to hear sirens any minute." Vince was standing again, hovering between the sofa and the window.

"It's Sunday afternoon, Vince, and this area is as dead as Connelly over there. Do you see the size of that hole in his head? It wasn't much more than a popgun, mate, probably sounded a lot like a car backfiring. Anyway, who around here is going to give a shit? I tell you, Connelly's going to have to smell a whole lot worse before anyone notices." On impulse I picked up a handful of the computer disks and stuffed them into the pocket of my fleece jacket. "There's more chance that the killer's still around. He could be waiting for us out there," I said, nodding past Vince's left shoulder.

He flinched away from the window. "Don't fuck me around, Nick. I'm scared, all right? I admit it. I've got no money, nowhere to go and I'm scared shitless."

I looked at him and he looked away. "No money? I thought you said you were still minted. You can't have got through six grand already."

"It's just bad luck. Fucking horses, eh?" He paused and coughed and tried to smile. I sighed and braced myself. "I need a loan, mate," he said. "That's why I dragged you here. I was going to try and touch him as well." He nodded at Connelly who was still staring patiently at the ceiling.

"Well, he's hardly going to turn you down, is he?"

Vince stared down at Connelly and slapped the palm of his hand against his forehead. "Of course. Connelly's money." He pushed the magazines to one side and rammed his arm between the cushions of the sofa. "Where the fuck is Connelly's money. Come on, Nick. Give me a hand. We'll go halves."

"I'm going to leave now, Vince. The smell in here is making me sick. And I'm not talking about Connelly."

"Get off your high horse. You can't leave me, Nick. It could be dangerous, you said so yourself. Hey, Nick. Wait!"

I closed the door behind me. I could still hear Vince's whining as I negotiated the small hallway and walked out into the street. I left him with Connelly for company. I think Connelly got the rough end of the deal.

It was the middle of February and spring seemed a long way off. The sky was low and seasonably grey. The wind was from the North and razor edged. I zipped my jacket up to the throat, hunched my shoulders and walked into the wind's teeth. The river was on my left and it smelt faintly of minerals and slightly more strongly of shit.

No matter, I felt good. I was aware that feeling good only minutes after discovering the murdered body of a former friend probably did not make me a nice person. I shrugged inwardly. Connelly was behind me, Vince was behind me. Ahead of me lay my small rented flat and, if I was lucky, a comfortingly tedious job in a warm, bland office somewhere. Perhaps I'd meet some proper people and form some close approximation of a normal relationship.

Yeah, right. And maybe shit doesn't stink.

*

When I'd first met Vince and Connelly a couple of years earlier they were dealing speed and ecstasy out of a squat on the Greenstead estate in Colchester. I'd been living rough for a while and was pissed six days out of seven. Vince and Connelly had got on the wrong side of a pair of squaddies outside a pub near the barracks and I'd stumbled to their assistance. Well, as I said, I was pissed. I took a punch to the head and a couple of decent shots to the kidneys, but I also earned the gratitude of a pair of lowlifes who recognised me as one of their own.

For the next eighteen months or so my bed was a sleeping bag on their kitchen floor. I worked hard at staying drunk and ran the odd errand for my new friends on the rare occasions that I lapsed into sobriety. Connelly injected himself with most of his profits and Vince's usually fell at the last or got beaten by a short head.

But eventually things began to dribble to an end. The local authority became more and more serious in their attempts to evict us. Connelly accumulated enemies with his usual legendary ease.

Then Vince's friend Mick offered to cut us in on a drug deal that he had stumbled upon during his last visit to London.

Mick was a borderline psychopath for whom Vince had done some favour's when they'd lived close to each other in Brixton a few years back. His reputation for casual thuggery was almost certainly exaggerated, but it was hard to find volunteers to test the theory.

If Mick was hovering near the bottom of the food chain then Kevin and Terry Mallon, identical twins from Liverpool, were many links below, scrabbling for scraps amongst the other dregs. They were long term heroin addicts and occasional Police informants who allegedly funded their habit by, amongst other things, procuring victims for a gang of child molesters.

The untimely demise of their closest acquaintance, a drug and pornography smuggler called Fielding, had left them holding a hundred grand's worth of China White. They put a little aside for a rainy day and agreed to offload the rest to a London based dealer. His name was Murphy and his brother was serving five years at Winston Green thanks to information supplied by the Mallon's. They wanted Mick to be their front man, expecting that Murphy would happily hand over forty thousand for the stash. Mick would get around two grand for his trouble.

The deal took place in a scruffy hotel off the Tottenham Court Road. The Mallon's weren't quite stupid enough to trust Mick, so they planned to watch from a safe distance.

Mick had other ideas. Vince, Connelly and I would get six grand each if we kept the Mallon's off Mick's back long enough for him to get away with the money. We all agreed to meet later at Liverpool Street Station.

Connelly took care of Terry Mallon. With trademark subtlety he smacked Mallon's head against a concrete pillar and kicked him several times in the bollocks.

Kevin Mallon watched the hotel from a cafe across the street. He sat in the corner drinking tea and smoking. I followed Vince into the cafe. I was hungover and everything seemed grey and veiled. I thought that perhaps we'd take a seat near Mallon, maybe create some sort of diversion when he tried to leave, keep him pinned down long enough for Mick to get away.

I didn't really know what to expect, but Vince surprised me anyway. He walked straight up to Mallon's table. Mallon stood, spilling his tea over the yellow vinyl. He started to speak, but Vince pulled a sock filled with snooker balls from inside his jacket and snapped it across the other man's face. Mallon's nose exploded in a pink spray and the back of his head smacked against the junction of the window and the wall.

Then Vince backed away, grabbed my shoulder and said, "Keep him here, mate. I'm going to make sure that Mick doesn't forget his friends." Before I could speak he'd disappeared into the afternoon's brittle warmth.

Mallon stirred. Two kids who'd been drinking Coke in the far corner stared open mouthed. The old guy behind the counter withdrew into a back room. I could smell my sweat and hear the rasp of my breathing.

Mallon tried to stand. Blood from his pulped nose had run into his mouth and he spat it out. He was gaunt and addict thin with long lank hair and wild eyes. He tried to come for me, but he caught the edge of the table and fell to his knees.

"Just forget it, mate," I said.

I was taller than him and more heavily built, despite my almost exclusively liquid diet. I didn't want to hit him. But then he came for me again so I did. It was a feeble roundarm right that caught him in the ribs. The state he was in it was enough to drive him back against the wall. Whatever wind he had left deserted him with a grunt.

I looked around the cafe. The kids were standing now and the old guy was back behind the counter. I decided to cut my losses and ran like fuck.

At Liverpool Street Station Connelly went berserk. "You let Vince go? Well, that's the last we'll see of him, you thick twat. Him and Mick'll be fucking miles away by now."

"It's only just gone three. They could make it yet."

"I'll give it ten more minutes, then I'm gone. By the way you tell it they got a good look at your face in that cafe."

"Yeah, I suppose they did."

Connelly covered his face with his hands. "Jesus Christ, Nick. You really are a useless streak of piss."

I must admit, I thought he had a point.

Then Vince came, walking briskly, a smug grin on his face, an Adidas holdall in each hand.

"About fucking time," Connelly said, "where's Mick?"

Vince looked away. "He decided he'd go up North. He knows some people in Leeds or Bradford or somewhere."

Connelly nodded. "I take it that's the money?"

"Already counted," Vince said. He passed Connelly the bag in his left hand. "This is yours and Nick's."

"Pillock doesn't deserve any. Nearly screwed the whole thing up."

"Just relax," Vince said. "It's worked out fine. Now, where the fuck are we going?"

146

Connelly glanced up at the nearest departure screen. "The next train from here goes to Norwich. No fucker in their right mind would go there, would they?"

"Sounds like the perfect place for us," I said.

No one spoke for a moment, then Vince shrugged and said, "Norwich it is, then."

*

"Call me George," George said, smiling.

I smiled back and shook his hand. He was bald with a ginger beard, but I didn't hold that against him.

"I found your CV most interesting," he said, with apparent sincerity.

I nodded brightly. My smile was starting to hurt a little. It was the Wednesday after Vince and I had found Connelly's body and we were in George's third floor office on Ber Street. The building was constructed almost entirely of glass and beyond George's head I could see the sun setting across a large chunk of the City, from the Cathedral, with it's spire encased in scaffolding, to the embryonic Riverside development and the floodlights of the football ground. The clear afternoon had yielded to a lurid dusk. Shades of salmon and lilac reflected fetchingly off the top of George's head.

He held up three blank sheets of paper. "Yes, most interesting," he said.

"I prefer the minimalist approach," I said.

He linked his hands behind his head and leant back in his chair. There were sweat patches under his arms. He wore a shirt the colour of pale mud with the sleeves rolled up and the top button undone. His erratically knotted tie was plain brown. I'm not entirely sure what it was made of, but I think polyester was in there somewhere. By contrast I looked pretty stunning in a crisp white shirt and almost clean, black 501's.

"Do you know how many people applied for this job?" George said.

I shook my head.

"Frankly neither do I," he said, "but it was a lot. I should know, I put most of them straight in the bin. Mostly graduates, of course." He rather cleverly made the word 'graduate' sound like 'scum sucking arsehole'. He knuckled his eyes wearily. "I haven't got time for this shit. I'm an engineer. A good one. I employ other engineers and draughtsman and they're bloody good too and I've got so much work I can pay contractors nearly thirty quid an hour and still make a hell of a profit."

"That's good, isn't it?" I said.

He frowned. "Yes, I suppose it is. The problem is these." He slapped the screen of the computer on his desk. Files and sheets of correspondence covered the keyboard. The rest of his desk was awash with faxes and sheets of calculations and the drawing board in the corner was piled high with box files.

"That's an old 486, isn't it?" I said.

He shrugged. "Dunno. Probably. Bit of an expert, are you?"

"Absolutely. Computer literate, that's me." I pointed to the label on the front of the hard drive. "Look, it says 486 right there."

George squinted at it. "Yes, I see. And that means something, does it?"

"Oh dear," I sighed.

"Precisely. I've got half the lads on CAD and half on drawing boards. I've got clients and architects wanting to e-mail me stuff and I've only just worked out how to use the fax machine. Apparently I need something called a file server and a web-site and Christ knows what else. Frankly, I don't know where to start."

"Sounds like you need one of those graduates you like so much. Or some IT whizkid looking for a change. Neither should be too hard to find."

"You're not exactly selling yourself, Nick."

I shrugged. "To be honest there's not much to sell. I want a job. Something routine and comfortable. But you seem a nice bloke, George, and I can't bullshit you. I've got nothing to offer."

George ran his fingers through his beard and nodded slowly. "On the phone you said something about a computer course that you're on."

"Yeah, it's pretty intensive stuff," I said, "first week we almost mastered the on switch."

George didn't laugh or even smile.

"I've read a bit as well," I said. I pointed at his computer. "I know that's an out of date piece of crap. And when you showed me round the office I noticed your boys were using low end Pentiums. They badly need upgrading."

"And this is the fellow with nothing to offer?"

"You don't get it. The blank CV was a gimmick, an attempt to be different, but it wasn't far from the truth."

He leant forward and drank some coffee from a Star Trek mug. He had the complexion of a farmer, not an office worker, with sunbursts of veins on his nose and cheeks. "Well, just humour me, then. Fill in the background a little."

I hesitated and he smiled encouragement. I could hear laughter beyond the closed door, from further down the open plan office. "You're a busy man. I'm wasting your time."

He sat back, still smiling. "I don't think so," he said.

I took a breath. I could hear the machine gun chatter of Alice, George's secretary, speed typing in the admin area. "OK," I said, "I'm twenty nine. I was bought up in Clacton and as far as I know my parents still live there. I haven't seen them for more than ten years. I studied English at Aston until I had a breakdown halfway through my third term." I looked down at my hands. "I seem to remember lots of nice people trying to help me, but they were wasting their time. I've lived rough or in squats or hostels since. That is, until I came to Norwich last summer. Now I live in a rented flat off Hall Road."

George shrugged. "So you've had a rough time. It sounds like you've put it behind you."

"Perhaps, but there are some things you should know. I've shared rooms with junkies and kids that sucked old men's cocks for a fiver a throw. Before I came to Norwich I lived with a paedophile and a drug dealer. I didn't know he was a paedophile at the time, but maybe if I hadn't been constantly pissed I might have picked up on some of the clues."

George looked at me, his face flat. "You had a drink problem?"

"I'm an alcoholic. I've drunk all kinds of shit. Meths, aftershave, anything with a kick."

"But you're not drinking now?"

"No. Not today."

"How long have you been dry?"

"Since I came to Norwich, about six months." I paused. "How about you?"

For a moment I thought I'd gone too far. George's natural good humour dropped from his face. Then the smile was back. A wry one this time.

"Eight years," he said. "Take one to know one, does it?"

"Something like that."

There was a brief silence that could have been awkward, but wasn't. I noticed that the sound of typing had stopped and I could hear raised voices from beyond the closed door.

George stood, frowning.

Then the door burst open and Alice, red faced, apologising, stumbled in. Behind her, like something from a nightmare, was Vince.

"Sorry, man. I know the timing's bad, but it's Carmen, she needs us. She's in trouble."

*

"Why Yarmouth?" I said. Vince and I were leaving Norwich on the Thorpe Road, heading for the bypass.

"Fuck knows," Vince said, taking a left turn without indicating. "Perhaps she went there when she was a kid. Feels safe there or something." He shrugged. "You know Carmen."

"Not as well as you, Vince," I said. He scowled at me. Carmen had been Connelly's girlfriend since just before Christmas, but Vince had always been sweet on her. Her real name was Tracy and she'd been bought up on the Larkman estate where she still lived, looking after her nine-year-old sister in a one-bedroom council flat. She called herself an exotic dancer, but we all know what that means. Still, it was a step up of sorts. Prior to that she'd turned ten-pound tricks to fund her heroin habit. But she was clean now, had been since her mother left, leaving her to look after Bethany.

"She's just a friend." He fingered his excuse for a beard with his left hand. "Mind you, with Connelly out of the way I could be well in."

"Right. The last time I saw the pair of you together she told you to fuck yourself."

"Just shows she cares," he said, "anyway, who is it she turns to when she's in trouble?"

"Poor girl must be desperate. What did she say exactly?"

Vince accelerated past an eight wheeler with the words Frettenham Lime Company printed on the side. "She's been getting calls. A couple before Connelly died, a couple after. A bloke with a Geordie accent threatening to kill her. He said loads of other stuff as well, apparently, but that was the bottom line."

"Why wait 'til now to do a runner?"

"The calls got worse, then someone put a brick through her window last night. She dropped Bethany with a friend and shacked up in a hotel in Yarmouth."

"And she called you?"

Vince nodded.

"Why?" I said, "no offence Vince, but how exactly are you supposed to help her?"

"I dunno," Vince said defensively, "bit of company, bit of moral support. The occasional shag. Maybe she thinks more of me than you realise."

"So why do you need me? I'd hate to be a gooseberry."

"Well, it could be dangerous, couldn't it? Perhaps I need a bit of moral support as well. I'd do the same for you."

I said nothing.

"And I'm sorry about that interview," Vince said, "but that George bloke seemed cool about it. Gave you his card, said he'd be in touch."

"Yeah, you make a great reference, Vince."

I stared out of the window. It was dark now and the fields and sky flashing past were merely different shades of ink.

"Looks better at night, doesn't it?" Vince said.

"What?"

"Norfolk. What a shit hole. Just like Kate Moss, flat and boring."

"I like it. It's understated. It's whatever you make it, like most things really."

Vince glanced at me, shaking his head sadly. "You've changed, Nick."

I looked out of the window again. "Thank fuck for that," I said.

*

I didn't become aware of Connelly's sexual tendencies until a few weeks after we came to Norwich. I suppose I missed several clues. I'm a drunk, that's my excuse, although it's no excuse for anything really. I'll have to live with the consequences, as will Carmen and Bethany.

When we lived in Colchester Connelly had a succession of women. He was good looking in a brutish kind of way and he usually had cash in his pocket and access to a variety of drugs. I didn't question it. I didn't question anything. Most of the women were older than him and most had children, daughters, between the ages of around eight and fifteen.

When we'd been in Norwich a couple of months I got a call from Vince. I'd seen little of him and Connelly. I'd paid six months advance rent on a flat in Trafford Street, I hadn't taken a drink and I attended AA meetings every day in a bleak church hall off Magdalen Road.

"It's Connelly," Vince said, "he's in hospital."

"What is it? OD?"

"No. He's been beaten up."

"Bad?"

"Could be worse. Fractured arm, badly bruised ribs, spoilt his looks a little. It's the old trouble again."

I did a mental double take. I hadn't really been listening. "What old trouble?"

There was a pause. "Come on, Nick. I'm not spelling it out."

"I don't know what the fuck you're talking about." I was irritated. I'd been planning my day, working out what course to enrol on, plotting twenty-four alcohol free hours. And I was halfway through a Mars bar.

"I know we're not good enough for you these days, Nick, but this is stupid. Just keep your trap shut if anyone asks any questions."

"What kind of questions?"

"For fuck's sake. Connelly was beaten up by a bloke called Bailey and a couple of his mates. He reckoned Connelly was fucking his ten-year-old niece. He denies it, but then he always denies it, doesn't he? Ring any bells yet, Nick?"

"No." I didn't want to think about it. Memories were stirring. I realised I wanted a drink.

"I don't believe you. He swore he was finished with all that shit. Burnt all his magazines, everything. All I know is that he's my mate and I'll stick by him. I don't expect you to understand that, Nick."

The line went dead. I looked out of the window and thought about the past and the future and ate the rest of the Mars bar in a single bite.

*

We drove past the Three Feathers pub on the Acle straight, approaching the outskirts of Yarmouth. Vince fiddled with the radio tuner, but couldn't find anything he liked.

"You have a go," he said. "Perhaps you can find a nice play on Radio Four. Something understated."

"Funny," I said, looking at him. He had on red tracksuit bottoms with purple piping and a frayed green sweatshirt. He was really making an effort. "Did you tell Carmen Connelly was dead?"

"No. Why?"

"Just wondered. There's something we're not saying here, isn't there?"

"What?"

"Bethany."

He gripped the steering wheel a little harder. We passed a caravan park and neared the roundabout that fed the town's one way system. "No way," Vince said. "He swore he didn't do that anymore. That's why he went on the Internet. He downloaded stuff. Sick stuff, I suppose, but all he did was look at the pictures."

"So that was all right, was it?"

"Saint fucking Nick. He was in a care home until he was sixteen, did you know that? They fucked him 'til he bled. Night after night, the poor bastard."

"That doesn't make it right, Vince."

He ran a hand through his hair. "No. Not Bethany. He swore on his life."

There was silence for a moment. "I'm sure he did," I said.

*

Vince parked his Escort in a Pay and Display off Regent Street. He unwound his window a little. The air that flooded in was vinegar sharp. He lit a cigarette and blew the smoke into the night. "There's something else," he said. "Something I probably should have mentioned earlier."

"It's about Mick, isn't it?"

He looked at me sharply, then looked away again. "Smart arse," he said. "Look, I couldn't resist it. Twenty two thousand quid, mate. I didn't feel like sharing. We took the back stairs out of the hotel. I took him out with the same sock and snooker balls I used on Mallon. I hit him twice. Couldn't risk him waking up while we were still around."

"Are you sure he wasn't dead?"

"I don't think so. Bet he had a hell of a skull ache, though."

"So we can add Mick to the list. But why do Connelly? Why not just take you out?"

"Probably thought we were in on it together."

"That's great, Vince. You must be some kind of prat. You've heard the stories about him, about the guy whose throat he cut because he looked at Mick's wife the wrong way."

"I asked him about that once. He said it was bollocks."

"Anyway, the bloke trusted you."

"Yeah, that surprised me as well. Still, it could have been Mick, or one of the Mallon's or someone else from Connelly's past, but I'll tell you one thing," he tossed the cigarette end out of the window, "it's got nothing to do with Bethany. I'd stake my life on it."

Which is pretty much what he did.

*

We met Carmen by a derelict church opposite a carpet warehouse in a backstreet a couple of miles from the front. The streets were deserted, but I thought I could smell the residue of a hundred Summer seasons; old chip and doughnut fat, Northern tourists, shoulders scarlet with sunburn.

Carmen was perched on a gravestone a few feet from the church's entrance. She had long black hair and dark eyes that had seen too much. She wore a three-quarter-length fake-fur coat with black gloves and boots. There was a gun in her right hand and it was pointed at Vince's head.

"It's all right, sweetheart, it's me," Vince said, walking slowly towards her, arms held out in front of him.

"What's he doing here?" she said, gesturing faintly in my direction.

"Thought we might need some muscle," Vince said. I could empathise with the look of contempt on Carmen's face, but it made me wince all the same. "You can drop the gun now." Vince said.

"You took the photo's, didn't you?" Her hand was shaking a little, but the gun was still pretty much centered on Vince's face.

"What photo's? What are you talking about? What's she talking about, Nick?"

"Bethany." I said.

She looked at me properly for the first time. "You'd better explain what you know about my sister. I'm just as happy shooting both of you. I'm way past caring."

Vince's mouth hung open. It was not a pretty sight.

"Vince didn't take the pictures, Carmen."

"How d'you know?"

"I've seen them."

There was a brief, charged silence. Carmen stepped away from the gravestone and moved towards us. Our breath turned to smoke in the cold air.

"What pictures?" Vince said.

Carmen and I stared at him in unison and our combined disdain was enough to silence him. She pointed the gun at me, eyes blazing. She was almost beautiful from a distance, but close up I could see the pock marks on her face and the flat loss in her eyes. I could smell her perfume and something else underneath it. "I turned Connelly's flat upside down looking for those photo's. I found his poxy camera, but that was all. No negatives, nothing. So how come you've seen them?"

"It's a digital camera, Carmen," I said. I pulled half a dozen computer disks from my jacket pocket. "The pictures you're looking for are on these."

"You took those from Connelly's flat on Sunday," Vince said.

"Almost," I said. "I went back and got these early Tuesday morning."

"You went back?" Vince said.

"Just give me the fucking disks and explain yourself," Carmen said, her face twisted. Her breath smelt of Spearmint gum and nicotine.

"Fine," I said, "just point that thing somewhere else and hear me out. If you still want to shoot me afterwards then fair enough. Frankly I'd rather be at home watching Coronation Street."

She let her arm drop to her side.

"What the fuck is going on," Vince said.

"I shot Connelly," Carmen said, "and I was going to shoot you too, you vile piece of shit."

"What?" Vince said. I think the penny was finally beginning to drop, but it was hard to tell.

"Bethany told me what that animal did to her," Carmen said. "She didn't want to, Connelly told her he'd kill her if she said anything. But I knew the signs. My stepfather first raped me when I was eight. I was sixteen before I told my mum. She told me to fuck off and leave her alone. So one afternoon when my useless junkie stepdad was asleep in his chair I stuck a syringe full of heroin in his arm. Even mum thought it was an accidental OD. My only regret is the bastard didn't suffer."

Vince was taking gormlessness to a new level. "You shot Connelly?"

"Not before he admitted everything that he'd done to Bethany. And I mean everything. I trusted that filthy bastard. Then he did it all to her again and this time he took pictures of it. Or rather he said that you took pictures of them, Vince."

"No way. I wouldn't do that."

"Why didn't you warn me, Vince? You knew what he was like. Why didn't you fucking warn me?" She put her hand to her face. I could see the tears now and I got the feeling they didn't come too often. "Poor little cow. She's gonna be more fucked up than I am."

"But he promised me..." Vince said, his voice tailing off. He stood with his shoulders slumped, staring at the ground. The wind came off the sea in small bitter gusts, chilling my face and feet. I wished I was at home, drinking vodka or whisky or strong lager. Or all three for that matter.

I tried to think of something else. I realised that both Vince and Carmen were looking at me. They seemed faded, beaten.

"Tell me what you know. Please," Carmen said.

*

After we'd found Connelly's body the previous Sunday I spent most of the night thinking about what Vince had told me about him. After my class at college on Monday evening I stayed on for a while and viewed the contents of the disks I'd taken from Connelly's flat. It was almost entirely pornography involving children between the ages of around six to fourteen years old. Boys and girls. There were also some animal shots by way of variety. I suppose about ninety percent was pretty obviously downloaded from the Internet and, God knows, that was bad enough.

The remainder, a dozen images on four disks, were pictures of Connelly and a blond girl no older than fourteen. They were taken in his flat. The enormous Sony squatted in the corner and Connelly's clothes were strewn over an arm of the sofa. There was a full ashtray on the floor and next to it, pathetically, were the girl's clothes in a neat pile by a bag of Haribo sweets and a Walkman.

When I turned the computer off my hands were shaking and my face was slick with sweat. It was as though I had a fever, a virus of some kind.

I lay awake that night, craving a drink, seeing the pain and fear on the girl's face and the dark glee in Connelly's eyes as he smiled at the camera.

*

"I went back to Connelly's flat yesterday," I said. "I wore gloves and wiped all the obvious surfaces the best I could. Have you got a record, Carmen?"

"What do you think?"

"Did you ever visit Connelly? Apart from Sunday."

"No. He always came to me."

"Good." I handed the disks to Carmen. "These are the only ones with Bethany on. I left a few of the others at the flat so the police know the kind of guy they're dealing with. I tied the rest in a bin bag with a brick and dumped them in the Yare."

"How did you know it was Bethany?"

"I picked her up from school once when Connelly couldn't make it. I think I'd have recognised her anyway. Long black hair, dark eyes that have seen too much. She takes after her big sister, doesn't she?"

Carmen stared at the disks in her hand and said nothing.

"She's not your sister, is she, love?" I said. "Who was it? Your stepfather?"

"It doesn't matter." She stuffed the disks into her coat pocket. "Thanks for these."

"By the way, where did you get the gun? A punter?"

She nodded. "He reckons it's untraceable. I'll dump it and the disks together." She looked at me. "Why are you so sure Vince didn't take the pictures?"

"The camera is reflected in the TV screen. There's nobody behind it. Connelly must have used a timer or something."

An elderly man walked past dragging a timid Yorkshire terrier behind him. The dog aimed a tiny bark in our direction then scuttled behind his master's legs.

I think we'd both almost forgotten about Vince. He leant back against a gravestone, his arms folded in front of him. "Well, this is very touching," he said. "I'm filling up over here."

"I think it's time to go, Vince." I said.

"Yeah? And who made you the piece of shit the world revolves around?"

"It's a bit late to find your guts, isn't it?" Carmen said, "you think I'm not going to shoot you?"

Vince shrugged. "I'm not sure I give a shit. One thing I want to know, though. Where's the money?"

Carmen looked at the ground. "What money?"

"Connelly's. He was into the kiddie stuff for kicks, but he was on the make as well. He had contacts in Holland and Belgium, dealing in video's and stills. He was going to start making his own videos. He was making cash hand over fist and I want my cut."

I think that if Carmen had shot him then I would have applauded.

"Just go, Vince," I said, "or I'll shoot you myself."

"You think I'm scared of you?"

"I'll make my own way back to Norwich. Get a train or something. I think I'd rather walk than get in a car with you. Just being in your company makes me want a drink."

"Well fucking have one then, you smug prick. Loosen up a little. You used to be worth knowing before you saw the light." He saw the gun in Carmen's hand and the look on her face. "All right, I'm going. Time I moved on anyway. My luck's been right out since I came to this hole. How about I give it a month or two and give you a ring? See how the land lies."

"I'd rather eat my own vomit than set eyes on you again." Carmen said.

"I'll take that as a no," Vince said, and turned and walked away. That was the last time I saw him; too tall, too thin, too ugly, stumbling into the darkness.

Carmen and I walked along the deserted front to her hotel. Amusement park rides loomed in silhouette. We passed forlorn hot doughnut stands and ice-cream stalls. She shivered by my side and said nothing. The air smelt of cold salt and uncollected rubbish bags.

Her hotel was called, with some originality, 'The Sea View'. It was small and shabby, but it was also one of the few open during the winter, so I don't suppose she had much in the way of choice.

In her room she took her coat off and lit a cigarette. She wore a burgundy velvet blouse and a black skirt. She sat cross-legged on the edge of the bed.

"It's in the wardrobe," she said.

The door was half-open; I pulled out a sand-coloured haversack and put it on the bed.

"How much?" I said.

"I haven't counted it. I can't keep it, can I? It's dirty money. I mean I've earned my living in some bad ways, but what Connelly did was something else."

The bag was full of different sized bundles of notes of all denominations.

"How's the dancing going?" I said, "I hear they might close down 'The Flamingo'."

"Yeah, fucking residents keep complaining." She hesitated and stared at the tip of her cigarette. "I've been turning a few tricks again recently. Just to keep my hand in."

"It's just money, Carmen. It doesn't know where it came from. There could be fifty or sixty grand in that bag. Take it. It's a fresh start for you and Bethany."

She turned away from me and gazed at the framed photograph of Derwent Water that hung over the bed. The room was grubby and cold and smelled of damp and loneliness. "I've killed twice, Nick, doesn't that worry you?"

"I don't think it's any of my business."

"Thing is, I enjoyed it. Especially Connelly. The more he begged the better it felt. When I pulled the trigger I nearly came in my knickers. The rush was up there with heroin. It was certainly better than sex, but then these are better then sex," she said, glancing at the cigarette between her fingers.

"He had it coming."

"You don't judge, do you, Nick?"

"It's one of my few redeeming features."

She looked up at me and then down at her hands as she smoothed her skirt across her thighs. "Vince was lucky, I nearly shot him before either of you spoke. God knows I wanted to."

"That stuff you fed him about threatening phone calls was just to get him out here?"

"Yeah. He wasn't hard to fool."

"Vince was never much of a thinker. How about the money? Are you going to keep it?"

She nodded slowly. "And what do you want, Nick?" she said, looking into my face.

Her eyes were a clear green and, if she wasn't beautiful, she was pretty enough, despite the pock marks and the sense of loss.

"About ten grand," I said.

She stood and stubbed out her cigarette in an ashtray on the dressing table. "Fine," she said, her mouth small and tight.

"It's not for me," I said.

"Of course not. I was starting to think you were different. More fool me."

"Believe what you like, Carmen. Look, it's up to you, you've got the gun."

She looked up at me with her eyes narrowed. Then she relaxed and started pulling bundles of cash from the haversack.

"Do you think we'll see Vince again?" she said as she counted.

"No idea. Does he worry you?"

"Not for a minute. I think I'll stay here tonight. I'll pick Bethany up in the morning and take it from there. What'll you do?" She glanced up at me briefly then turned back to the money.

"Catch a train, hitch a lift. I'll get back to Norwich somehow."

She stopped counting for a moment. "You could stay here the night."

I fiddled with the zipper on my jacket. "Thanks, but I've got to get back."

She nodded, her face turned away from me. "I mean I wouldn't charge you or anything."

"That's sweet," I said, my voice thick. I hesitated, trying, and failing, to remember the last time I shared a bed with a woman. "I'm sorry, I can't."

"No problem," she said, looking up at me, her smile a little too bright. She shovelled the counted money into a Sainsbury's carrier bag and handed it to me.

I thanked her and we said our good-byes, awkwardly, without touching. I was glad when I walked out into the night, throat dry, face burning in the cold air.

A couple of days later I was at home, watching 'The Simpson's', dunking dark chocolate digestives in a cup of strong coffee when the telephone rang. I snapped "yes" into the receiver.

"Have I called at a bad time?" George said.

"Sorry. It's been a strange week. And I'm watching 'The Simpson's'."

"I used to record that for the kids. Homer's my role model."

"Good choice."

"I'm calling about your interview. I'm offering you the job."

"Really? And you seem so sensible."

"I thought a three month trial? See how we go?"

"Fine," I said.

"I'll see you Monday morning, about nine. Sort out the details."

"Actually George, can we make it Tuesday? It looks like it's going to be a long weekend."

I sensed rather than heard the sigh. "Tuesday then. Don't be late."

I thanked him again and hung up.

It was Sunday evening before I caught up with Mick in 'The Nelson', a real bucket of blood near the Tottenham Court Road, about half a mile from the hotel where Vince had blind-sided him the previous Summer. He was sitting in the stuffy, crowded bar, drinking a pint of Guinness. I think I saw the condensation beading his glass before I saw him.

He wore a black leather jacket with a pale green sweatshirt and biscuit coloured combat trousers. His eyes widened briefly when he saw me. He was thick set and had a deceptively pleasant face with a neat black goatee beard and close-cropped hair.

He smiled and said, "What'll it be? The usual? Don't tell me," his brow furrowed, "pint of Stella and a whisky chaser."

"I'll have an orange juice. Thanks." I said.

He tipped his head to one side, tucking the smile away for a moment, making sure I wasn't taking the piss.

"Fine," he said. He held out his hand and I shook it. "You look good, Nick."

I took my drink and thanked him.

"You were a drunken pile of shit the last time I saw you."

"You're making me blush," I said.

"So," he said smiling, "what the fuck are you doing here?"

I passed him the canvas sack in my hand. "Settling a debt," I said. "I don't want to be looking over my shoulder the rest of my life."

"It's Vince's debt, not yours. Give me some credit, I'd worked that much out. I was a prat to trust that git. I was going to settle with him in my own time." He looked at the bag.

"How much is there in here?"

"About ten grand."

"Better than nothing," he said, "but I'm still twelve thousand down."

"It's the best I can do."

He shrugged. "What the hell. I'd written it off anyway. I was going to catch up with Vince some day, when he wasn't expecting it, but I'd given up on the cash." He drained his pint and squinted at me. "I appreciate this, Nick, but what's in it for you?"

"Nothing really," I said, "Just want to make sure we're straight. And I'd leave Vince to rot, if I were you. He's not worth the effort."

"You want me off Vince's back, don't you?"

"It just seemed the right thing to do, that's all."

He shook his head and chuckled to himself. "You've changed, man."

"So I'm told."

"What happened? You find God or something?"

"Not exactly. I've found him a little elusive."

He asked about Connelly and I told him.

"I heard he was into that shit. Pity the fucker didn't suffer a bit," he said.

"Have you had any come back from the Mallon's?"

"You must be joking. Terry's dead, fuck knows where Kevin is." He saw the surprise on my face. "Yeah, that China White they had was the real thing, completely pure. The shit they were used to was cut with all sorts of crap. Terry took the first hit and he may as well have walked in front of a train. Kevin did a runner and he's not been heard of since. With a bit of luck he'll go the same way as his brother."

I drained my glass. "I've got to go, Mick."

He nodded. "As I said, I appreciate this. If you need anything get in touch."

We shook hands again and I walked out into the night.

*

On Friday there was a report in The Eastern Daily Press concerning the discovery of the body of a suspected paedophile and drug dealer in a bedsit on Riverside Road. The police were appealing for information.

*

I got the telephone call three weeks later. I was at work, helping a bloke called Stuart install the latest detailing software. It was a learning experience for both of us. Jane, our receptionist, put the call through to me on Stuart's phone.

I recognised the voice, the Liverpool accent, the moment he spoke, even though I'd only heard it once before in my life.

"How's it going, Nick?" Kevin Mallon said. "I've got a friend of yours here. He's not feeling too well." The line crackled with static, but I could still make out Vince's voice in the background, half-sobbing, half-begging.

"Where are you?" I said, trying to keep my voice steady. But Stuart must have sensed something, because he glanced sharply up at me, eyebrows raised. I gave him a thumbs up and an attempted grin and he turned back to his computer.

"We're on top of a car park, mate. Multi-storey. Cracking view, isn't it, Vince? Fuck. I think the dirty bastard's pissed himself. Sorry about the crap line. It's Vince's mobile. Cheap and nasty, just like him."

"Where's the car park?"

"You'll find out soon enough. We're quite close to the edge now, aren't we mate? Stand up, Vince. Yeah, I'm cold as well. He can't stop shaking, fucking wimp."

I could hear Vince's muffled shouts. "Just hold on, Mallon," I said, "don't be stupid." Stuart was looking at me again and the rest of the office seemed to go quiet beyond the screens around his desk.

"I'm way past stupid," Mallon said. His voice had an edge to it now and his accent thickened. Static hissed, the sounds of struggle in the background seemed to intensify then halt abruptly. "Who'd have believed it? Vince can't fly."

"You're a piece of shit, Mallon. You'll go the same way as your brother."

"You think I give a fuck about Terry? I needed that money. Now I need to get even. I hear some bitch did Connelly for me. That just leaves you and Mick."

"You may as well follow Vince down, do everyone a favour."

162

"In your dreams. Hey, it's been nice chatting, but I've got to go. It's going to be busy around here soon. And don't worry, mate. I'll be in touch," he said and broke the connection.

I put the receiver down and wiped the sweat from my face. The office seemed hot and close.

"You all right, Nick?" Stuart said. "You look as white as a sheet."

"Fine, thanks," I said, managing a smile of sorts. "It was just some wind up merchant. Nothing to worry about."

Stuart shrugged uncertainly. I sat next to him and tapped the monitor. "Right then. Where were we?" I said.

After work I watched a film at 'Cinema City'. It was in black and white and had sub-titles and half an hour after it had ended I'd forgotten the plot. If, indeed, it had a plot. As I walked home the cold wind harried me around every corner and drove the rain in bitter gusts. Over the weekend I left a message on Mick's mobile warning him about Kevin. Monday morning I was back at work. The wind was still bitter, the rain cold.

But it didn't matter much. Despite everything, spring was coming.

Previously from Elastic Press

The Virtual Menagerie by Andrew Hook

In this collection of nineteen surreal stories Andrew Hook rides the slipstream through a series of fantastic yet familiar scenarios skating the twilight zone of our own imaginations.

Unsettling dissections of the mind - Nicholas Royle

Forthcoming from Elastic Press

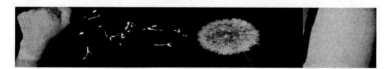

Second Contact by Gary Couzens

Exploring the twin themes of time and identity Gary Couzens manipulates our sensibilities in a major collection of nineteen powerful stories, drawing on the fascinations that dwell within the hearts of us all.

For further information visit:

www.elasticpress.com